WHO'S THAT GIRL?

Miss Tyler moved on ... announcement. There was a twinkle in her eye as she glanced at the paper. 'This one's really boring,' she said, 'but I'd better read it out anyway. I don't suppose anyone here has heard of Rory Todd?'

Becky couldn't believe her ears. Could there be anyone in the world who hadn't heard of Rory Todd? He was only the most gorgeous pop star in the entire universe.

'Some of you may know that a few years ago Rory was a student here at Bell Street,' Miss Tyler continued. 'And in three weeks time he wants to come back to film his new video here, and he and the video director think it would be a good idea to have some Bell Street pupils appearing in the video with him. Apparently they want a crowd of students dancing in the background . . .'

Becky was still trying to take in the amazing news. 'I don't believe this is happening!'

Liz nodded. 'I know, it's like a dream.'

'But it's not a dream!' Becky laughed. 'It's really true!' And more than anything she wanted to appear in the video with Rory Todd. But how on earth was she going to do it?

Coming soon in the Bell Street School series:

I'm No Angel
Mystery Boy

Who's That GIRL?

BELL STREET SCHOOL

1

HOLLY TATE

Knight Books
Hodder and Stoughton

British Library C.I.P.

A catalogue record for this book is
available from the British Library

ISBN 0-340-55957-8

Printed and bound in Great Britain
for Hodder and Stoughton Children's
Books, a division of Hodder and
Stoughton Ltd., Mill Road, Dunton
Green, Sevenoaks, Kent TN13 2YA.
(Editorial Office: 47 Bedford Square,
London WC1B 3DP) by
Cox & Wyman Ltd, Reading

1

'I've lost my pens – and I can't find my notes anywhere. It's no good! My first day at college is going to be a complete disaster!'

Becky Burns looked up from her bowl of cereal, a gleam of amusement in her blue eyes. 'Calm down, Dad! There's no need to get into such a state. Your lecture notes are in your briefcase, where you put them last night.'

'And your pens are in your jacket pocket, where you put them ten minutes ago,' added Susie, Becky's step-mother. They exchanged a long-suffering glance across the kitchen. Mr Burns had been up at half-past six that morning and hadn't stopped panicking ever since.

'I'd better just go and check everything again,' he muttered and disappeared once more.

'Peace at last,' Susie said with a sigh, bringing a plate of toast to the table. 'How about you, Becky? You seem very calm. If I was in your position I'd be feeling nervous.'

'I am,' said Becky. 'In fact I'm—' But before she could add the word 'terrified', her father was back again.

'What about my tie? Do you think I'm too dressed

up? Maybe I should just wear a casual shirt and jacket . . . '

Becky shook her head. This was getting beyond a joke! 'You look fine, Dad. Now sit down and have some breakfast. I've never heard such a fuss!'

'I should have known understanding and sympathy were too much to ask for,' he grumbled good-naturedly, sitting down all the same. 'It's all right for you, Becky. You don't have to start a new job today.'

'No,' replied Becky, putting down her spoon. 'It's dead easy for me,' she said with heavy irony. '*I* just have to start a new school.' She pointed to the pink and purple Bell Street badge on her navy sweatshirt. 'I won't know a single person there – and I don't even get paid for going! But do you see me getting into a panic?' She raised her eyebrows.

'I'm sorry, love.' Her father looked sheepish. 'I'd forgotten it was your first day, too. Bell Street's a nice school, though. You've got nothing to worry about.'

'Oh, no?' Becky's face darkened. The thought of walking into a classroom of strangers made her shiver. 'Maybe I'll hate it there,' she said. 'Or maybe the other kids won't like me.'

Mr Burns put his arm round Becky's shoulder and gave her a hug. 'You know that isn't going to happen. You had lots of friends at your old school.'

Becky sighed. If making new friends was her only problem, it wouldn't have been so bad. But there was something worse than that troubling her. Something that had kept her awake for hours the night before.

'What if they find out about the Kelly Kid?' she asked.

Her dad shook his head. 'You're not still worried about *that*?'

Becky nodded. How could she *not* be worried? The Kelly Kid was one of the reasons she'd decided to take up her dad's offer to live with him and Susie when they moved north to Wetherton. Here she had the chance to make a new start, away from people who knew about her past and the Kelly Kid. But what if someone at this new school recognised her? What if they started to pick on her and make her life a misery, just like some of the kids at her old school?

'Becky, no one's going to know you were the girl who starred in those terrible Kelly's Krunch adverts!' Mr Burns laughed.

'They might work it out.'

'Just look at you.' Her dad pointed to her reflection in the mirror on the wall opposite the breakfast table. Becky gazed at her smooth blonde hair. A pair of bright blue eyes stared back at her from a pretty, heart-shaped face.

'You see,' said Mr Burns. 'The Kelly Kid had ginger hair in braids and freckles and bright red cheeks. Unless you go giving the game away by tap-dancing and singing "I love Kelly's Krunch", no one's going to guess that you were the Kelly Kid in a million years!'

Becky tried to smile, but it was difficult. 'What am I going to do if they do find out?'

Mr Burns shrugged and pulled a face. 'You left the Kelly Kid behind in London. At Bell Street you're just ordinary, boring Becky Burns.'

'Yeah, you're right,' said Becky. But somehow she didn't believe it.

'Hold on a minute – it's the postman!' Becky jumped out of the back of the car and went to collect the mail as the postman came up the drive.

'Anything exciting?' Susie asked as Becky climbed back into the car. 'Or is it just bills and junk?'

Becky sorted through the envelopes until she came to one with an Air Mail sticker. 'All junk except for one – and that's for me,' she exclaimed, tearing it open.

'From New York?' asked Susie, backing the car down the drive. But Becky was too busy reading her mother's letter to reply. For a while Becky had thought her mother had forgotten that she was starting at Bell Street School this week. Sometimes her mother was so busy with her acting career that she didn't have time to remember things that were important for other people. But she hadn't forgotten this time. *'I hope to have some exciting news for you soon,'* she'd written at the bottom of the page. *'Meanwhile, lots of luck and fun in your new school. I know you'll make friends there. Missing you like mad! I'll call you soon. All my love, Mum.'*

Becky read it twice and then, feeling much more cheerful, put it back in the envelope and tucked it into her backpack. It was like a good luck charm, she thought.

Susie parked her car outside the school gates, squeezing in among the other parents delivering their kids. There was a long drive with trees each side that led up to the school itself. From the front,

Bell Street School looked old and attractive, built of red bricks and with big white windows divided into smaller panes. When they'd come to view the school, Mr Burns had been very impressed and said it was Georgian. But beyond this old part, there were modern concrete and glass extensions. Becky didn't really care what the school looked like, as long as she was going to be happy there.

Susie was watching the students walking past and heading up the drive. Most of the girls were wearing navy skirts or trousers and jerseys, but some were wearing brighter colours. 'It doesn't look as if they're too strict about clothes,' she observed.

Becky nodded. She'd noticed, too. 'Maybe I'll wear my navy and white striped shirt tomorrow,' she mused. 'I prefer it to the school sweatshirt.'

Susie turned round to face her. 'Are you sure you don't want me to come in with you?'

Becky hesitated for a moment, then shook her head. If her mother had been here she would have said yes, but somehow with Susie it was different. Susie was nice, but Becky felt she didn't want to rely on her too much. She didn't want Susie to think she could replace her mother. 'It's okay, I know what to do. I'll go and report to the school office.'

'All right.' Susie looked anxious. 'Have you got everything?'

Becky giggled. 'Yes. I'm better organised than Dad!' That made Susie laugh.

'Well, have a really good day. I'll see you this afternoon.' Becky slid out of the back seat, slammed the door and watched as Susie drove away. Then she turned, took a few deep breaths and joined the

9

other kids walking up the drive. *Bell Street School,* she thought to herself, *here I come!*

'This is Becky Burns. Becky's just moved here from London,' Miss Tyler explained to the students of 2K.

Becky stood in front of the class and felt a shiver run up her spine at the sight of all those eyes staring at her. What were they all thinking? she wondered. Suddenly she felt very lonely and helpless. How would she manage in this new place? Becky bit her lip and concentrated on Miss Tyler, who wore glasses with bright red frames and a bright red sweater and lipstick to match.

'I can remember how confusing everything was when I first came here, Becky,' said Miss Tyler, 'so I'm going to team you up with someone who'll show you around for the first few days. Liz, would you look after Becky?'

'Sure.'

Becky glanced across the room to where Miss Tyler had been looking. A girl with shining, light brown hair tucked smoothly under a velvet band smiled and pointed to an empty seat at the desk next to her.

Becky gratefully slid into the place, noticing that Liz's desk was neatly piled with books and her pencil and pens were laid out in a tidy pattern. In fact everything about Liz was neat and tidy. Even her plain white blouse looked as if it had been starched and ironed just two minutes earlier.

Becky sank down in her seat. It was a relief not to have everyone looking at her. And it wasn't just because she felt shy and nervous. After all, someone with sharp eyes and a good memory for faces might just have recognised her as the dreaded Kelly Kid.

'Hi,' Liz whispered as Becky sat down. 'My name's Liz Newman.' She had nice hazel eyes and a friendly smile. And a friendly face was just what Becky needed right now. 'Just stick with me and I'll show you the ropes.'

'Thanks.' Becky managed a nervous grin. 'I was getting scared about finding my way around.'

'Don't be scared about that; you'll soon learn. And I'll introduce you to some of the others later.'

Becky was relieved. If everyone in the class was like Liz, she had nothing to worry about!

'We've got a lot of announcements to get through this morning, so I'd appreciate your attention,' Miss Tyler said when she'd finished taking the register. She ran a red pencil down the list. Red was obviously her favourite colour, Becky thought. Something told her she was going to like Miss Tyler.

'The first thing is the summer fête, which is held the Saturday after next. As usual every class is going to have its own stall to raise money for charity – so we need to come up with a brilliant idea for ours.'

There was a long silence. 'Nothing?' Miss Tyler asked with a surprised smile. 'I thought we might be able to come up with at least one idea.'

'How about a raffle?' someone suggested.

'Or a junk stall?'

Miss Tyler looked disappointed. 'We could do either of those, but I was hoping we could do something more original and exciting. Let's all think about it. Perhaps we can come up with something

11

that will make the whole school wish they were in 2K too.'

'Maybe we should have a stall selling nothing but red things!' whispered a quiet but strangely husky voice behind Becky. She turned round to see a mischievous looking girl with dark eyes and very short black hair, almost like a boy's. She looked like a naughty pixie.

'Don't be wicked, Jas!' Liz said with a giggle.

Becky couldn't help laughing. 'Miss Tyler would buy everything, wouldn't she?' she whispered.

Miss Tyler was already on to the next announcement. There was a twinkle in her eye as she glanced at the paper. 'This one's really boring,' she said. 'I don't suppose any of you will be interested, but I'd better read it out anyway. I don't suppose anyone here has heard of Rory Todd?'

Becky couldn't believe her ears. She threw up her hand – and so did everyone else in the room.

Miss Tyler laughed. 'I thought you might.'

Could there be anyone in the world who *hadn't* heard of Rory Todd? Becky wondered. He was only the most gorgeous pop star in the entire universe. Every night in her bedroom at her mum's house she'd drifted off to sleep with his handsome face staring down at her from all four walls. And she owned every single record he'd ever made.

'I really like Rory Todd, don't you?' asked Liz.

'Like him?' Becky widened her eyes. '*Like* him? I'd do anything in the world to meet him!'

'Well maybe you'll get a chance, Becky,' said Miss Tyler, making motions for the class to settle down. 'Some of you may know that a few years ago Rory was a student here at Bell Street. And in three weeks' time he wants to come back to film his new video here.'

Becky could scarcely believe her ears. Rory Todd was an old Bell Street student – and coming back here? She felt as if she was going to burst with excitement. And everyone else in the room seemed to feel the same way.

'Calm down, everyone,' said Miss Tyler. 'If you're not quiet, you won't hear the rest of the news.' There was instant silence. 'Rory Todd and the video director think it would be a good idea to have some Bell Street pupils appearing in the video with him. Apparently they want a crowd of students dancing in the background . . . '

'Well you can count me out of the video,' called a boy from the back of the class. 'I hate Rory Todd.'

'Ryan Bryson's an idiot,' Liz said dismissively. 'He wouldn't know good music if he heard it.'

Becky was still trying to take in the amazing news. 'I don't believe this is happening!' Her heart was beating like a drum.

Liz nodded and her hair shimmered round her face. 'I know, it's like a dream.'

'But it's not a dream!' Becky laughed. 'It's really true!' And more than anything she wanted to appear in the video with Rory Todd. But how on earth was she going to do it?

2

'Come and meet some of the others,' Liz suggested, leading the way to one of the tables in the dining area that lunchtime. As Becky carried her tray across the room the noise seemed to echo round the high ceiling and deafen her. So many people – and she didn't know a single one of them! The strangeness of the place began to overwhelm her, and she suddenly felt shy and awkward. If only she could be back at her old school . . .

'This is Jasmine Scott,' Liz introduced.

Jasmine was the girl with the short, black hair and cheeky face Becky had noticed earlier that morning. 'There's no need to be so formal, Liz!' she exclaimed in her strangely husky voice. She sounded years older than she looked. 'Hi, Becky. Call me Jas, like everyone else.'

Becky smiled as she sat down. Jas looked as if she could be fun.

'And I'm Charlie,' said the girl next to Jas. 'Or Charlotte Farrel, if you want my full name.' Charlie peered at Becky through the wire-rimmed glasses perched on the end of her nose. They made her look serious and rather arrogant.

'Hello. I noticed you in class,' Becky said, nodding. It was difficult not to notice Charlie. Not only did she wear those glasses, but she had three long tie-dyed scarves fluttering around her neck and a flowing black skirt that almost reached the ground. And then there was her hair, which was bright red and hung halfway down her back. No, thought Becky to herself, it would be difficult to forget Charlie once you'd seen her!

Right now, Charlie was looking closely at Becky's plate. 'Have you got bacon in that sandwich?' she asked disapprovingly.

'Yes, it's a BLT – bacon, lettuce and tomato.'

'I don't know how you could eat it. Have you any idea of the conditions most pigs live in?' Charlie frowned.

'Charlie's a vegetarian,' Liz explained. 'She takes it really seriously – *and* she tries to make us feel bad when we eat meat.'

And she's succeeded, thought Becky, suddenly losing her appetite. She wasn't sure she and Charlie were going to get along. There was something about Charlie's superior attitude that Becky didn't like.

'We were just talking about Rory Todd and planning how to get into the video,' said Jas.

'I think Rory Todd is just too much.' Liz sighed and picked up a neat slice from her pizza. 'I wish I knew how to get into that video.'

'I'm not really into Rory Todd,' admitted Charlie, polishing her glasses on one of her scarves. 'But I read that he's given some money to an animal sanctuary, so I wouldn't mind being in his video. I think I'll design a special Rory Todd T-shirt and print it up in the art class. That should catch his eye when he arrives.'

'Getting him to notice us – that's the problem.'
Jas frowned and took a packet of chewing-gum from
her backpack. 'I think I'll buy something really great
to wear, something that'll knock him out.'

Becky, who'd been admiring Jas's black mini-skirt
and scoop-necked white top as they sat there, wasn't
surprised. Jas was obviously into fashion in a big way!

'I don't know what I can do,' mused Liz. 'I wondered
about making some badges, but I'm not sure that'll
impress him.'

Becky's mind had been racing while they talked.
'I've just had a great idea,' she said excitedly. 'Miss
Tyler said Rory wants people to dance in the video,
so I'm going to start working on a dance routine!
Then when Rory arrives and auditions people, I can
really do something impressive.'

Liz looked up. 'That *is* a great idea! I wish I was
good at dancing.'

Becky almost smiled. It was impossible to imagine
Liz having a hair out of place, let alone getting hot
and sticky on the dance floor!

But she could see herself now, the lights and
cameras all focused on her as she danced with Rory
Todd. Maybe she could sing with him, too. And
afterwards he'd invite her out and—

Charlie interrupted her daydream. 'Hold on a
minute, Becky,' she said sharply. 'You're new here.
You're not a proper Bell Street student. Rory Todd's
coming back here because he wants local kids in
his video – not someone who's just moved from
London. It wouldn't be fair if you were chosen.'

Becky's eyes widened with alarm. She couldn't
believe what Charlie was saying. 'But I'm good at

17

dancing and singing. If Rory's looking for people to dance, then I should have a chance of being chosen. I was the star of a—' She cut herself off just in time. She'd been about to tell them that she'd been the star of a TV advert, and that would have got her into all kinds of trouble.

'What did you star in?' asked Liz with interest.

Becky flushed. 'The school play,' she said quietly. It was true. She *had* starred in a play at her old school, but it didn't sound quite as impressive as saying that she'd appeared on TV. 'It was *The Wizard of Oz* and I had to sing and dance,' she argued. 'Everyone said I was really good.'

Charlie's serious expression didn't shift. 'You may be a brilliant dancer and singer, Becky, but that's not the point. You're a stranger here. It wouldn't be fair on all the other kids who've been at Bell Street for years if you just walked in and got a place in the video. Imagine how you'd feel if you were in our position. You'd think it was really unfair.'

Becky felt her mouth go dry. For a moment she couldn't think of a thing to say. Until a few minutes ago everything at Bell Street was going fine. Now suddenly it had all gone sour. 'I don't think *you're* being fair,' she said at last with quiet determination. 'I may be new here, but I've got just as much right to be in that video as anyone else.'

There was a long silence. Liz and Jas looked down at their plates, obviously embarrassed. 'What do you think?' Becky asked Liz.

'I can understand your side of the argument,' Liz said slowly, going bright red. 'If I were you, I'd feel the same way. But Charlie's got a point. There are some people who'd get really upset if you got a place in the video and they didn't. I'm sorry.'

'So you see, Becky,' Charlie concluded, 'it would be better all round if you just forget about appearing with Rory Todd.' And with that she picked up her lunch tray and carried it over to the trolley.

'Don't take any notice of Charlie,' advised Jas, offering Becky a piece of gum. 'She's always getting on her high horse about something or other. She'll get over it.'

Becky took a piece of gum, but it was going to take more than chewing-gum to make her feel better. Inside she felt hurt and confused. The worst thing of all was that Charlie did have a point. If Becky just barged in and grabbed a place in the video, it was going to put an awful lot of backs up. What was she going to do? Forget about the video and concentrate on making friends? Or set her sights on appearing with Rory Todd – and risk becoming the most unpopular girl in the school?

By the time the last class ended that day, Becky was looking forward to going home. But when the bell went the science teacher, Mr Harris, asked her to stay behind while he found some notes for her. When she eventually emerged from the classroom everyone else had disappeared and she didn't know which way to go. How on earth was she going to get out of there?

She set off down one of the yellow corridors with classrooms opening off each side. Displays of work were pinned along the walls, but Becky hardly noticed. A set of stairs went down to the left, but she felt sure she hadn't come up that way. The corridor ended in a set of swing doors. She pushed them open. Another corridor turned off to the right.

Becky looked around for some familiar sign, but there was nothing. She was beginning to panic when a deep voice stopped her in her tracks.

'Becky! What are you doing here?'

Becky sighed with relief as she saw Jas walking towards her. 'Thank goodness!' Becky exclaimed. 'I thought I was never going to escape.'

'It's confusing when you first come here,' Jas agreed, chewing a piece of gum. 'If you can wait a few minutes, I'll show you the way out. I've got to put up some posters.' She unrolled one and began pinning it to a noticeboard. 'Actually, I think it might interest you.'

Jas had evidently been busy in the art department. Written across the top of the poster in splashy red paint Becky read the words ELECTRIC PORCU-PINES. 'What's an Electric Porcupine?' she asked.

'The Electric Porcupines are a band,' Jas grinned, rolling the remaining poster up. 'I'm the lead singer. The others in the band are from Bell Street too. We sometimes practise here and we play at school dances and things like that.'

'Are you any good?' Becky didn't intend to sound rude. Somehow the question just slipped out.

'Of course we're good!' Jas exclaimed. 'We're the best band in the school.' For a second her cheeks reddened. Then she laughed and added, 'I'd better be honest and admit we're the *only* school band at the moment. There used to be a rap group and a heavy metal band, but they've broken up.'

'So what's this all about? Are you advertising a gig?' Becky stepped back so that she could read the poster.

'We're looking for a new backing singer,' Jas explained. 'That's why I thought you might be interested. At lunchtime you said you can sing and dance. Maybe you're just the person we need.'

'What would I have to do?' Becky asked.

'Nothing too terrible. For a start, you have to come to the audition and sing for us. Then you'd have to learn our songs and come to rehearsals – and gigs, of course.' Jas shouldered her backpack and led the way out, down some steps and through the main hall. Then they came to the school entrance.

'See you tomorrow. Think it over and let me know what you decide,' Jas called as she left Becky and went off to put up another poster. 'The band could do with a bit of livening up!'

'I'll think about it,' Becky called as she walked out of the door. It was tempting. At any other time she'd have jumped at the chance to join the Electric Porcupines. Singing in a group was something she'd always wanted to do. But somehow it didn't seem as exciting today as it might have done the previous day – not in comparison with appearing in a video with Rory Todd. Right now nothing in the world seemed to matter quite as much as that . . .

'It sounds like an amazing first day!' said Susie when Becky had finished telling her everything that had happened.

Becky suddenly jumped up from the sofa. 'Is it okay if I call a couple of my friends in London? I want to tell them about Rory coming to Bell Street!'

'Well . . . ' Susie looked at the clock on the mantelpiece. 'Can you wait for a couple of hours? It'll be cheaper then. London's a hundred miles away and long-distance calls are expensive at this time of day.'

Becky couldn't hide her disappointment. If she called later, her friends might have gone out. 'Just one call now?' she asked. But Susie shook her head. 'I guess I'll go up to my room, then,' Becky said coldly. She stamped up the stairs noisily, not caring what Susie thought.

Her room was at the front of the house, overlooking the road so that she could watch people coming and going if she wanted to. It was quite an old house but the people who had owned it previously had modernised and redecorated it. Becky's room was large and had a big built-in wardrobe and wallpaper covered in tiny pink and green flowers.

Although the room was pretty, somehow it didn't feel like home. Becky looked around at the bare walls. There was something missing – and she knew exactly what it was. She opened the wardrobe doors. On a shelf was a big blue plastic tube. She took it out, pulled off the lid and gently slid the contents on to her bed. One by one she unrolled her posters. Each of them showed Rory Todd's handsome face and flashing green eyes. Just seeing him made her feel better.

But what was she going to do with the posters? When Becky had first arrived, Susie had said that the wallpaper was too pretty for her to cover up. Becky began to feel even more furious. This was

22

her room, not Susie's! Defiantly, she opened one of her desk drawers and took out some sticky-putty.

It took a long time to decide where to hang each picture and put it up on the wall, but when she'd finished Becky stood and admired her work. Rory's face stared back from all four walls – and suddenly the room felt as if it was really hers.

A tap on the door made Becky jump.

'Becky, supper's ready, and your dad's home.' Susie's head of curly brown hair appeared round the door. Her smile faded as she caught sight of the posters.

'What do you think?' Becky asked, pretending she hadn't noticed. 'It's beginning to feel like home in here, isn't it?'

Susie bit her lip. 'I thought we'd agreed that you wouldn't put any posters up in case you damage the wallpaper.'

'I changed my mind.' Becky held her chin in the air.

'Well, I'm not sure it's a good idea. Your room looked so fresh and pretty before, and now you've covered it in pictures torn out of magazines.' Susie waved her hands in the air. 'It's a real mess!'

Becky was speechless for a moment. But then a wave of anger swept over her. 'It's my room,' she shouted, 'and *I* like it this way!' She turned her back on Susie so she didn't have to see her, and she heard the door shut.

Oh, why had she ever agreed to come and live here? But there was nowhere else for her to go now that her mother had gone to America. Nobody really wanted her around. Not her mum, certainly not Susie . . . She wiped away the tears that had begun to trickle down her cheek.

'Come on, Becky, tell me what's wrong.' She hadn't heard her father come in. He put his arms round her and gave her a long hug. 'Susie told me you'd had a really nice surprise at school,' he said, pulling out his handkerchief and giving it to her to wipe her eyes. 'So why the tears?'

'It's Susie!' Becky mumbled, blowing her nose. 'Nothing I do is right. She doesn't want me to have my posters on the walls.' Mr Burns looked round. 'Well,' he said with a shrug, 'I think we can persuade her that it's up to you what you stick up in your own room, don't you?' Becky looked up at him. He was smiling in that funny, crooked way that always made her want to laugh. 'So long as you don't insist that we have pop posters all over the rest of the house. Is it a deal?'

'It's a deal.' Becky managed to smile through the tears. 'But what's Susie going to say?'

Mr Burns looked thoughtful. 'We'll just have to talk it over with her. It's going to take time for us all to get used to living together, but we'll manage it, I promise.'

Becky shivered. She hoped they could work it out, because if they couldn't, there was nowhere else for her to go.

Her father let her go and sat down. 'What's this Susie was telling me about Rory Todd coming to the school? I expected you to be really excited about it. Or have you gone off him?' he teased.

'No!' Becky protested. 'When Miss Tyler told us he was coming to the school it was wonderful. But then some of the other kids, well, Charlie, really, started getting at me because I was new.' She told him the whole story.

'And it's all so unfair!' Becky finished despairingly. 'I know I've got a good chance of being chosen to appear in the video with Rory, but the others want to stop me even trying.'

Mr Burns looked puzzled. 'Perhaps they're a bit jealous. Maybe they think you've got a better chance of being chosen than they have.'

'Maybe,' Becky agreed. 'My idea of making up a dance routine was more practical than theirs.'

'So in a way you can understand why Charlie wants to rule you out of the competition,' her father suggested.

Becky thought about it. Perhaps he was right, but what help was that to her? 'What am I going to do about it?' she asked, annoyed. 'If they feel jealous, they're not going to want to be friends with me.'

'Why not just play it cool?' Mr Burns leaned back on the bed. 'Look at it this way: it doesn't really matter what Charlie says, because when it comes down to it, Rory Todd himself will choose the kids *he* wants to appear in the video. And if he chooses you, there's nothing Charlie or anyone else can do about it.'

'I suppose that's true,' Becky admitted.

'Meanwhile, why not try and give the impression that you're not too concerned about it? That way the other kids won't feel you're trying to muscle in on the situation, and you can make friends with them.' Her father raised one eyebrow. Becky didn't know how he did it; when she tried it, both hers rose together.

'Yes,' she agreed. 'You're right. If I just keep quiet, maybe Charlie will stop glaring at me through her glasses as if I've done something wrong.'

'Well, I'm glad we've got that particular problem cleared up,' Mr Burns said lightly, getting to his feet. 'Now let's go downstairs and have some supper and sort out this poster problem.'

'Do I have to?' Becky groaned. She still felt sore about Susie, even though her father seemed to be on her side about the posters.

'Yes,' insisted Mr Burns. 'Let's talk it over.'

'All right.' Becky wasn't exactly happy about it, but her dad was probably right. 'I'm just going to wash my face before I come down.'

'See you in a minute then.' He left the room.

Becky looked at herself in the mirror. Though her eyes were red from crying and her hair was all in a mess, she felt much better. Tomorrow she'd go into school and play it cool. She wouldn't waste her energy on arguments with Charlie or the others. She'd save all her efforts for Rory Todd. And when he arrived she'd show everyone at Bell Street what she could really do!

3

Although she'd made up her mind to play it cool, as Becky walked up the school drive the next morning she realised that she was the only one who had. Everyone else had gone Rory Todd crazy! As she rounded the side of the building and entered the playground, she could hear the sound of Rory's music blaring from tape players.

Looking round, she spotted Liz and Jas and a couple of other girls from 2K sitting in the sun on the bank of grass that sloped down from the playground to the sports field. She went over to join them. All of them, she noticed, were wearing Rory Todd badges.

'Hi there!' Liz called, squinting into the sun as she waved. She looked just as neat and tidy as she had the day before, and she was resting a clipboard on her knee. 'Have you any ideas for our stall at the fête? I'm making a list.'

'Come and save us, Becky,' groaned Jas, making space for her to sit down. 'Liz is trying to get us organised.' She pulled a glum face, but with her sparkling dark eyes and boyish haircut, she just looked cute.

Liz flushed. 'Well, someone around here has to be organised! I'm not trying to be bossy, if that's what you think.'

'We know.' Jas patted her arm. 'Just teasing you.'

'That's a great picture of Rory,' Becky said admiringly to Liz, pointing to a badge that Liz had made herself. 'Where did you find it?'

'It's from last month's *Chart* magazine.' Liz sounded surprised. 'You mean to say you didn't see it? There was a brilliant article all about that song of his, "Mystery Girl".'

'I love that song,' murmured Jas. 'It's on this tape. Hold on.' She fast-forwarded until she found it.

'I think this is my favourite song,' Becky said dreamily as Rory's deep voice began to sing. 'I play this over and over again. I like to think I'm the mystery girl he's singing about.'

'You can't be,' Liz protested with a twinkle in her eye. 'Didn't you know *I'm* his mystery girl? I'm sure he saw me walking up Wetherton High Street one day and wrote this song about me.'

'You're both wrong,' Jas insisted with a wicked grin, 'because he's singing to me!'

They all roared with laughter.

'When he comes here, maybe we could ask him who the real mystery girl is,' Liz suggested when they'd calmed down.

'I don't want to know,' said Jas, taking a piece of chewing gum from the packet she always seemed to carry with her. 'I'd prefer to go on dreaming that it's me.'

'Mystery girl don't run away from me . . . ' Rory sang the chorus and Becky joined in. Jas listened for a few moments, then came in too, harmonising with Becky. They sang together till the end of the song.

'That sounded really great!' Liz's eyes shone. 'Oh,

I wish I could do that,' she added wistfully.

Jas was looking at Becky appreciatively. 'Our voices go well together, don't they? Have you thought any more about what I was saying yesterday?' But before Becky could reply one of the other girls gave a shriek.

'Look over there! Clinton Walsh is wearing a Rory Todd baseball cap. I wonder where he got it from.'

'And just look at Ryan Bryson!' exclaimed Liz.

Becky recognised Ryan as one of the boys from 2K. Except that today he looked nothing like the boy she'd seen yesterday. He'd swapped his navy sweatshirt and trousers for black jeans and a black leather jacket covered in studs, like the outfit Rory Todd wore on the cover of his *Surrender* album.

'I don't believe it,' Liz said crossly. 'Didn't you hear him saying how much he hated Rory yesterday? He said he wouldn't appear in the video even if Rory begged him. Now just look at him, trying to show off!'

Jas shook her head. 'Miss Tyler's going to go bananas when she sees him like that!'

'Here comes Charlie!' Liz pointed across the playground. 'Look, she's got some Rory badges too!'

Becky, who'd been feeling so relaxed, felt her stomach churn. She hated to admit it, but she was scared of Charlie and her bad temper.

But Charlie seemed to be in a better mood this morning. She even smiled at Becky as she sat down. She was dressed even more strangely than the previous day. Her hair was in a loose ponytail and she was wearing a pink rose tucked into the scarf she'd tied it up with. 'No badges?' she asked, looking at

Becky's unadorned shirt. 'I thought you said you were Rory's number one fan.'

'Well,' Becky said slowly, remembering the previous night's conversation with her dad, 'I thought about what you said yesterday and I've decided to play it cool. None of us know who Rory Todd is going to choose to appear in his video, so I'm not going to worry about it. You can count me out of all the fuss.'

Charlie pushed her glasses back up her nose. 'I'm really pleased you see it that way, Becky. I've been feeling bad about what I said yesterday. I was a bit hard on you. But I'm glad you're not upset about not being in the video. Now we can get to know each other and be friends.'

'Us too,' said Liz and Jas together.

Becky just smiled. Yes, it would be good to have them as friends. But as for giving up her hopes about the video – she hadn't said a word about that, had she?

'It's down here.'

Late for history class, Liz and Becky hurried down the corridor, turned a sharp corner – and walked straight into Emma Pennington, who fell flat on the floor.

'I'm sorry!' Becky bent down to pick up Emma's bag, while Liz helped her up.

'Are you all right?' Liz looked really worried. 'Are you hurt? Is your leg okay? God, I hope we haven't done you any damage.'

Emma seemed fine. She got to her feet and smoothed her dark blue skirt.

Becky hadn't really taken much notice of Emma before. Liz had pointed her out, but there was nothing really to notice about her. Everything about her had seemed quiet and a bit plain. She wore a sensible navy blue skirt and sweater and her dark hair was cut short. In class she seemed reserved, though she was good at answering the teachers' questions.

She smiled at Becky, who was looking concerned. Becky was surprised to see how Emma's face lit up. She was the sort of girl who was pretty in a shy, rather special kind of way. 'Don't worry about it. I'm not made of glass, you know! We'd better hurry up if we're not going to be late for Happy Heyward's lesson.'

'Why do you call him Happy?' Becky asked as they got going.

'Because he's the most miserable teacher in the whole school!' Emma grinned, and her face lit up again.

Liz shook her head. 'No, he's the most miserable teacher in the world!'

Becky raised her eyebrows nervously. 'I don't think I'm going to like history from the sound of it.'

'Don't worry; it's not so bad,' Liz reassured her. 'He's normally okay. It's only when he's in one of his moods that he's really nasty.'

'Let's hope he's having a good day,' Emma muttered as they reached the classroom door in the nick of time.

But he wasn't. 'Uh-oh,' whispered Liz as she took one look at his face. Mr Heyward was incredibly tall and thin, with a pale face and lots of wild black hair that seemed to be standing on end. His eyebrows were so low they met in the middle of his face, like a thick black line. 'That's a bad sign,' she murmured. 'Watch out!'

'I think I've seen him before – in a horror film,' Becky whispered as she sat down at a desk next to Jas. Yes, there was something distinctly spooky about him.

Mr Heyward stood with his bony hands on his hips and stared at them ominously. Becky felt the hair on the back of her neck begin to prickle.

'Before the start of the lesson I want to make one thing clear,' he said in a voice like thunder. 'You're here to learn history, and while you're in this room I don't want to hear a single word about Rory Todd. I'm sick of hearing about him! One mention of his name and the whole class will have a detention.'

Jas's eyes widened. 'There'll be trouble,' she whispered.

'What was that?' Mr Heyward stalked over to Becky's desk.

'Nothing, sir.' He frowned at her and Becky shivered. But then his face softened a bit and he seemed almost human.

'You must be the new girl.' Becky nodded and gulped. 'Well, I'm pleased to see that you're not covered in badges,' he said. 'Unlike everyone else.' Charlie's badges and the rose in her hair had caught his eye. 'Take those off, Charlotte. And the greenery, too. And you, Jasmine, and everybody else here. Take off all those badges and put them away. And, Jason, if you don't remove that baseball cap immediately I'll confiscate it.'

'Now,' said Mr Heyward, when every sign of Rory

32

Todd had vanished, 'let's get down to the Spanish Armada. I want you to imagine you're Sir Francis Drake . . . '

Once he started to talk about his favourite subject, the atmosphere in the classroom began to improve. It even became fun. 'He's not so bad after all,' commented Becky, who was drawing a map showing the route taken by the Spanish fleet. On the other side of the room Mr Heyward was busy showing some of the other students pictures of different kinds of warships.

'Forget history.' Jas shaded the coastline of her map in blue. 'You haven't told me whether you're going to audition for the Electric Porcupines yet.'

'I haven't made up my mind,' said Becky, telling the truth. She hadn't really thought about it since yesterday. She'd been more concerned about making up with Susie, who'd agreed Becky could keep her posters on the walls of her room, and phoning her friends in London who'd been green with envy when they heard about Rory's visit.

'Well, I hope you will audition.' Jas looked concerned. 'Please think about it, Becky. There's only one other person who's shown any interest and that's Kirsty Gregory, the lead guitarist's girlfriend. She's got a terrible voice, like a cat wailing!'

'Does she sing like this?' Becky gave a yowl, as if someone had trodden on a cat's tail.

Jas exploded in giggles. '*Just* like that!'

'What's going on here?' Mr Heyward had crept up on them. 'I told you, girls, I don't want to hear any singing or talk about that ridiculous pop star.'

'I wasn't talking about Rory Todd,' Becky protested. 'We were just saying . . . '

But it was too late. Mr Heyward's eyebrows had come down into a thick black line across his forehead. His cheeks went as white as the chalk. 'Didn't you hear me say that I didn't want to hear that name mentioned in this room?'

'But I didn't mean— It wasn't . . . ' Becky spluttered.

But it was too late. 'Right, 2K,' thundered Mr Heyward. 'I want to see every single one of you here after school on Thursday for a half-hour detention. Remember to tell your parents you'll be late home. And if anyone misses it, I'll see you all on Friday, too.'

A ripple of protest went through the room.

But Mr Heyward was not in the mood for listening. 'If you want to complain,' he snapped, 'you can do so to the young lady sitting there.' And his finger pointed directly at Becky. Twenty furious faces turned in her direction.

'I'm supposed to be having a riding lesson after school on Thursday!' someone hissed furiously. Becky turned to see Gina Galloway glaring at her. Gina was a very pale girl with a cloud of fluffy hair like yellow cotton wool. She was also, according to Liz and Jas, the most stuck-up girl in the class. This was the first time she'd bothered to speak to Becky.

'I'm sorry,' Becky said coolly.

'Riding lessons are expensive, I've a good mind to make you pay for it,' Gina snapped before turning away.

Becky shut her eyes. She felt terrible. If only the ground would open and swallow her up. That had to be better than being the most unpopular girl in the whole class.

'Don't worry about it,' said Liz for about the millionth time.

'I just feel so stupid.' Becky sighed. 'Half the kids in the class aren't talking to me. Oh, it's awful!'

It was the lunch hour, and the four of them – Liz, Jas, Charlie and Becky – were lying on the grassy bank where they usually gathered. The sun was beating down and they were half-shaded by one of the silver birch trees dotted along the bank.

'Oh, cheer up,' ordered Jas, hitching up her short skirt another few inches so that her legs would tan. 'Happy Heyward was out to get someone and he just happened to pick on you. Don't take any notice of the moaners. They're just glad it wasn't them who caught it.'

Suddenly she grabbed Becky by the arm. 'Hey, don't look now, but I think your luck's just about to improve. Someone's watching you.'

'Who? Don't tell me it's Mr Heyward on the warpath again.' Charlie peered through her glasses and did a double-take. 'Oh, wow! Daniel Armstrong! And he's coming this way.'

'Who's Daniel Armstrong?' Becky forgot about detentions and history and turned round to see who was the cause of all the excitement.

Liz went pink. 'He's only the best-looking boy in the fourth year – and he's nice, too.' She smoothed her hands over her hair and adjusted her velvet band.

'I never knew you fancied him!' Jas teased.

'Well, you've got to admit he *is* handsome,' Liz retorted, brushing a couple of bits of grass off her skirt.

Becky had to agree with her. Daniel Armstrong was tall, with dark brown hair and the kind of smile that reminded her of Rory Todd. And he was staring straight at her as he walked over to them! She tossed her hair back from her face and tried to pretend that she hadn't noticed him.

'You've obviously made a big impression,' Jas whispered in her husky tone. 'It's definitely you he's interested in.'

Becky sat up and gave him a dazzling smile as he approached her. He nodded to the others and Liz went a deeper shade of pink. 'Hi,' he said to Becky.

'Hi.' She gazed long and deep into his eyes. They weren't quite as green as Rory Todd's, but they were still a pretty impressive hazel colour.

'My friends were telling me you're new here.'

'Yes, yesterday was my first day.' Becky tried to make her voice sound calmer than she felt. 'I'm Becky Burns, by the way.'

'Right.' He was looking at her steadily, as if he couldn't quite believe what he saw. Becky felt her heart do a somersault. But before the conversation could get more interesting, the school bell sounded, summoning them all back for their next class.

Daniel frowned, as if he'd wanted to say more. 'I was just – well . . . Look, I've got a chemistry class, so I have to go now. But I'll see you around, Becky.'

'Yo!' breathed Jas when he was out of earshot. 'Did you see the way he was looking at you? No doubt about it – he's burnin' up for Burns!'

Charlie was playing with a strand of red hair. 'Looks as if you've made a big impression,' she murmured approvingly. 'Lucky thing!'

Liz smiled. 'Gina Galloway is going to be even madder than ever! She's been after Daniel Armstrong for ages!'

Becky felt a thousand butterflies fluttering in her stomach. Maybe Bell Street wasn't such a bad place after all. Forget detentions and horrible Happy Heyward . . . suddenly it was a lovely day!

4

'*And now it's all up to – you-oooh* . . . ' Becky finished
the song with a flourish, then turned to face her
audience and gave a bow. 'How about that? Did I
get it right all the way through?'

Jas bounced up and down on Becky's pine-framed
bed. 'Yeah, you've got it! And it'll be even better with
the band playing, too.'

'It's a good song,' Becky admitted, putting down
the sheet of paper on which Jas had written the
words.

'It's the best of the Electric Porcupines' songs.'
Jas admired herself in the mirror above the dressing
table and struck a pose. 'I really like this pink lipstick
of yours. Do you mind if I borrow it some time?'

'This one's even better. My mum gave it to
me.' Becky outlined her mouth with a bright red
lipstick and pouted. 'There. I wonder what Daniel
Armstrong would say about me now?'

Jas looked disgusted. 'Forget Daniel Armstrong!
The only thing you should be thinking about is
that audition tomorrow. Wait until the band hear
you sing – they'll ask you to join on the spot. I
promise.' She took a bright red chiffon scarf they'd
found in one of Becky's drawers and tied it round
her head in a bow. 'Just think – when we're both in

the band we can do dance routines and plan some amazing costumes. It'll be great.'

Becky felt confused. She wasn't sure whether she wanted to be in the band or not. On the one hand, it might be fun like Jas said. On the other hand . . . She sighed. It was difficult to explain. Being so new to the school, she didn't know what she was getting herself into. She really liked Jas, but she didn't want to spend all her time with her. There were bound to be lots of other things to do and other friends to make. But how could she explain that to Jas?

'Where did you get this? It's wicked!' Jas picked up a big straw hat that had been hanging on the wardrobe door. She strode up and down the room like a catwalk model.

'That was my mum's,' Becky admitted. 'I, er . . . liberated it from her wardrobe when she went off to New York.'

'Your mum's in New York?' Jas looked surprised. 'Wasn't that your mum unpacking all those boxes in the living room?'

'No!' Becky laughed. 'That's my step-mother, Susie. My mum and dad got divorced a few years ago and my dad married Susie last year.'

Jas was quiet for a second. Then she asked, 'I can't imagine my mum and dad splitting up. Don't you mind?'

'Yes, of course I do.' Becky frowned. Talking about her parents still hurt. For a long time after the divorce she'd hoped her mother and father would get back together again, but she'd had to forget that when Susie had come on the scene.

She tried to smile, but it was hard. 'There's nothing I could do about it, though.'

Jas took off the hat and sat down on the bed, looking subdued. 'I'm sorry, Becky,' she murmured. 'I didn't mean to pry.'

'That's okay. It's good to talk about it.' Becky wrinkled her nose. 'At the moment I'm not getting on very well with Susie.'

'Don't you like her?' Jas's dark eyes flashed. 'I don't think I'd like it if my dad got married to someone else.'

Becky stretched her arms over her head. 'She's nice – or at least she tries to be nice. It's just that she's not used to kids. That's what my dad says, anyway. He says it'll take time for us to get to know each other.'

'So why has your mum gone to America?' Jas asked.

'She's an actress. She's got a part in a TV show over there.'

Jas gasped. 'Wow! Is she famous?'

'Not really. Her name's Vanessa Warren.' Becky was careful. Her mum wasn't exactly a movie star and people sometimes felt disappointed if they hadn't heard of her. 'You might know her face if you saw it.'

'Have you got a photo of her?' Jas asked.

'Yeah. I've got some albums.' Becky opened the pine chest she'd brought from her old room in London. She hadn't unpacked all her stuff properly yet and finding things was a bit difficult.

'Have you met any film stars?' Jas asked, leaning over her.

'Not really.' Becky stacked some books and old clothes on the floor. 'She does mainly stage plays and TV dramas, though while she's in America she said she might have a go at getting into a film.'

'I wish my mum was an actress,' Jas said wistfully. 'Hey, Becky, if she goes to Hollywood, perhaps you could go and see her there.'

'Yeah, maybe.' Becky tried not to think of things like that. Her mum was great, but her life was very hectic. One day she was in London doing a television drama, the next she was on tour for months doing a play. It had been all right before the divorce because her dad had been around to look after Becky. But after that – well, life with her mum had been exciting, but it wasn't exactly reliable. That was one of the reasons Becky had decided to come to Wetherton. She hoped it hadn't been a big mistake.

At the bottom of the chest she found her photo album. Jas came and sat on the floor to look. 'That's Mum,' Becky said, pointing to a photograph. 'And here she is again with me.'

Jas looked closely. 'I'm sure I've seen her on TV. Wasn't she in a murder mystery series?'

'Yeah,' Becky nodded. '*Crime of Passion.*'

Jas was turning the pages. Suddenly she stopped and gave a loud screech. 'Yuck! Why have you got a picture of the Kelly Kid in here?' She took the album out of Becky's hands. 'God, I hated that girl!'

Becky's blood ran cold. She'd forgotten all about that photo! Her mum had seen a poster of the Kelly Kid in the street one day and for a joke had insisted on Becky posing in front of it. It was her mum, too,

42

who had stuck the picture in the album. 'One day you'll be proud of it,' she'd said. Becky had just tried to forget the whole thing.

'That was just a joke,' she muttered, trying to sound nonchalant even though her heart was beating like a drum. 'I hated the Kelly Kid too.' She went to turn the page, but Jas stopped her.

'What a laugh!' she crowed. 'You know, whenever the Kelly Kid came on TV doing that stupid dance I used to throw a cushion at her. And that song!' She put the photo album on the bed and stood up. 'How did it go? "I am the Kelly Kid and I love Kelly's Krunch." That's it!'

Becky gulped. Jas had got that lispy, little-girl voice almost perfect. It made her feel sick. Suddenly she felt as if she was right back there in the TV studio with the director bullying her into making a fool of herself in front of the camera. 'Come on, Becky,' he'd told her. 'The Kelly Kid is the kid everyone loves to hate. You *do* realise that, don't you?' But Becky hadn't realised. She hadn't understood that they were going to make fun of her until it was too late.

'Are you all right?' Jas interrupted her thoughts. 'You've gone really pale. You know,' she added a moment later, 'there's something funny going on here . . . ' Her voice trailed off. She took another look at the photograph. 'It's not you, is it, Becky?'

'*Me?*' Becky tried to sound innocent, but her expression must have given her away.

'It is, isn't it?' Jas shook her head in disbelief. 'You're the Kelly Kid, aren't you? Your face is the same under that wig and the make-up.'

'Don't be silly!' Becky tried to pull the album away, but Jas held on to it.

'It's true!' she stared at Becky, wide-eyed. 'I can't believe it!'

'Just don't tell anyone, all right?' Becky said quickly, slamming the album shut.

'Why not? Don't you want people to know you've been on TV?' Jas looked confused.

'As the *Kelly Kid*? You're joking! At my last school everyone made fun of me. That's one of the reasons I wanted to come here – to get away from the Kelly Kid.' Becky bit her lip. 'Look, please, Jas, don't say anything. Let's just keep it a secret.' She raised her eyebrows. 'Please?'

'Okay, if you want.' Jas shrugged.

'Yes, I do.' Becky felt desperate. If this got out, she didn't know what she'd do. It would ruin everything! She took a deep breath. 'Look, Jas, I've been think-ing about the audition tomorrow and I definitely do want to be in the band.' It wasn't strictly true, but perhaps it would encourage Jas to keep her secret.

'That's great!' Jas grinned. 'I knew you'd make the right decision.'

Becky gritted her teeth. In the circumstances, what choice did she have?'

'I'm going to get you!' The Kelly Kid's sickly sweet smile dissolved into a horrible snarl revealing a set of sharp fangs. She reached out and Becky noticed that her fingers ended in gleaming steel claws. With a loud scream, her heart pounding with terror, Becky began to run down the dark corridor that stretched ahead of her. It seemed to go on for ever, twisting and turning like a maze. And always, behind her, she could hear the Kelly Kid's footsteps and cackling laugh.

Then suddenly the corridor came to an end. A door stood open and she ran through it, panting and shaking with fear, and slammed it shut. She'd escaped! With a relieved laugh she turned around – only to find a tall, thin figure with the whitest face she'd ever seen and two big black beetles where his eyebrows should have been, glaring at her. 'Welcome to my history class,' he hissed, 'from which there is no escape!' And then his hand fell on to her shoulder and he began to shake her and shake her until she felt her head was going to fall off . . .

'Becky! Becky, wake up! You've overslept.'

Becky opened her eyes. 'Don't shake me. I've come for detention,' she muttered, still half-asleep.

'You'll get another detention if you don't wake up!' Susie said, laughing. 'Come on, love. I've brought you some orange juice.'

Becky opened her eyes slowly. Her heart was still beating overtime.

'I had a terrible dream,' she groaned, untangling herself from the duvet and looking around the room. Rory's face smiled down reassuringly at her and brought her back to reality. She glanced at the alarm clock by her bed, which should have gone off fifteen minutes ago. 'Oh, no!' She leaped out of bed and headed for the bathroom.

Miss Tyler was just about to call the register when she finally raced into class. 'You're cutting it fine!' she said cheerfully, taking out one of her red pencils.

'I thought you weren't going to make it!' Jas

exclaimed as Becky slid into her seat. She winked and pressed her finger to her lips, as if promising that they were sealed.

'Now,' said Miss Tyler, who looked like Mrs Santa Claus in her red blouse and bright red tights. 'We talked about the school fête earlier this week and I asked you for some bright ideas for a stall. Let's have some suggestions now, please.'

There was silence. 'We could fill a big jar with sweets and then ask people to guess how many of them there are,' Mina Chotai suggested. Mina's parents ran the sweet shop near the school. She had a glossy black plait that hung down her back to her waist.

'Thank you, Mina. That's a possibility, but perhaps we could think of something that everyone could join in with.' Miss Tyler smiled encouragingly. 'Nothing else?'

'We could bake cakes and sell them,' Emma Pennington said softly.

'Well I'm not baking cakes,' said Ryan Bryson.

'Thank goodness for that,' Miss Tyler replied smoothly. 'We don't want anyone dying of food poisoning, do we, Ryan?'

The rest of the class laughed and Ryan's face began to redden.

'Ryan's terrible at home economics,' Liz explained to Becky. 'We made Cornish pasties a few weeks ago and he didn't cook his properly. It made him sick when he ate it.'

'Well, keep thinking about the fête, won't you.' Miss Tyler looked worried. 'We'll have to think of something, but right now I have another announcement about Rory Todd.'

46

Instantly the room went silent.

Liz gasped. 'Don't say he's not going to come!'

'Yesterday there was a bad attack of Rory Todd-itis throughout the school, as I'm sure you all noticed,' Miss Tyler said sternly. 'I believe there was an outbreak of it in your history lesson.'

Becky stared at her shoes. She'd hoped Miss Tyler wouldn't get to hear about the detention. Perhaps the whole school knew. She felt more embarrassed than ever.

'Some of you,' continued Miss Tyler, 'seem to think that the more you cover yourselves with pictures of Mr Todd, the more chance you'll have of appearing in the video he's going to make here. I've been asked to tell you that this is not the case.' She said the last five words very slowly and clearly.

Liz and Charlie, who were both wearing badges, looked at each other in alarm.

'The school staff had a meeting last night and decided that we couldn't bear hearing any more of Rory Todd's songs or confiscating any more badges and posters,' Miss Tyler explained. 'So we've decided that we will choose two people from each class to appear in the video.'

There was a gasp. 'You can't do that!' Charlie complained loudly.

'Oh yes we can,' said Miss Tyler. 'The head teacher has spoken to Rory Todd's video director and he's agreed to let us select pupils to appear in the video.'

'But who are you going to choose?' asked Clinton Walsh.

Miss Tyler surveyed the whole class. 'Rory Todd

will be coming here in exactly three weeks. So I'm going to choose the two people who contribute most to the class in the next two weeks – the two most positive, most helpful pupils.'

Jas looked horrified. 'This means we're going to have to be on our best behaviour all the time!' She quickly took out her chewing gum, which she wasn't supposed to chew inside the school buildings.

Becky listened to everything and began to feel even more fed up than before. She'd got the whole class a detention after only two days at school. What chance did *she* have of being chosen to appear in the video? None at all, after a start like that. A black cloud of disappointment hung over her.

'Oh, and I have some good news for Jasmine,' Miss Tyler continued. 'When Rory Todd was a student here he played in a school band. The video director thinks it would be a nice idea to feature a current school band in the video – and as the Electric Porcupines played at the last school dance, the head teacher would like them to appear. I know you sing with the band, Jasmine, so congratulations.'

Everyone in the room turned to stare at Jas, whose smile seemed about a mile wide. And Becky began to grin too . . .

'This could be our big break!' Jas and Becky were waiting in line outside the maths room for the first lesson of the day and Jas could hardly stand still, she was so excited. 'If we can impress Rory Todd we might end up with a record contract!'

'Just think – the Electric Porcupines at number one in the charts!' Becky felt faint with excitement at the thought of it. She still couldn't believe her luck. For a few minutes all hope of appearing in the video had seemed to vanish. And then suddenly she was back in with a chance.

Jas laughed. 'Good job you decided to audition for the band, Becky!'

Becky gave a wry smile. It was strange how things turned out. If Jas hadn't found out about the dreaded Kelly Kid, Becky might have said no to the audition. And then she would have looked a real hypocrite if she'd suddenly changed her mind after Miss Tyler's announcement!

'Once you're in the band,' Jas went on, 'we'll have to make some changes. For a start, we've got to decide how to knock Rory Todd dead when he comes. The boys won't listen to me on my own, but with two of us . . . '

Becky's mind was racing. 'We could do one of Rory's songs. How about a version of "Mystery Girl"? That would really make him listen.'

'Yeah. And we'll need to think about clothes and make-up,' mused Jas.

'We'll give the boys a make-over, too. Maybe they could just wear black – black jeans and black shirts. That would look great.'

Jas waved a finger at her. 'That comes later. Just remember to turn up at the gym during lunch break.'

'I'm not going to forget,' Becky promised. No, it would take a stampede of elephants to prevent her from getting to the audition. Thank goodness she'd decided to bring some casual clothes to change into. She couldn't sing properly in her school uniform.

To think that just half an hour ago she had been cursing Jas for getting her into this situation. Now there was no way anyone was going to stop her auditioning and getting a place in the band. From here on in, it was going to be easy!

5

Becky checked herself over in the mirror in the girls'
changing room. She'd slipped out of her school
uniform and into some black leggings, with a long
shirt and brightly patterned waistcoat over the top.
Her hair was tied up into a bunch on top of her
head and her lips were pink and shiny with lipstick.
Goodbye, Becky Burns, schoolgirl, she said to herself as
she twirled in front of the mirror, *and hello Becky B,
pop star!*

From outside the gym she could hear the ampli-
fied sound of guitars being tuned. Becky paused,
waiting to make her grand entrance so that Jas and
the other members of the band would be impressed,
then flung back the door – only to discover that the
gym was packed. There was hardly room for anyone
to move. Even Jamie Thompson, the quiet boy who
sat a couple of seats along from Liz, had come
along.

Becky stared round in amazement. What were
they all *doing* here? Jas had said no one was interested in auditioning.

'Hi, Becky,' a voice called. It was Emma Pennington,
perched half-way up the wall bars so that she had a
good view of what was going on. 'I love your outfit.
Have you come to audition too?'

'Jas asked me to come,' Becky explained. 'What are all these people doing here? I thought I was going to be the only one.'

'They're auditioning for the band. After this morning's announcement, practically everyone in the school who can sing is having a go.'

'Are you?' Becky asked, surprised. Surely Emma was too reserved to sing in a band.

'No!' Emma gave an embarrassed laugh. When she smiled, her face, which was normally so serious, was transformed. 'I've just come along to watch. Gina and Charlie are auditioning and so is one of my friends from another class.'

At that moment Liz came squeezing through the crowd. 'Here you are, Becky! Jas sent me to look for you.' She looked up at Emma in amazement, 'Are you sure you're okay up there? Why don't you come down, Emma? It's safer.'

'I'm not going to fall off, I promise, Liz.'

Becky sensed that Emma was annoyed. She didn't really blame her. Liz was treating her like a little kid. It was really strange.

Emma suddenly pointed over their heads. 'Look, Gina's going to sing now.'

As she spoke, the band began to play. Becky recognised the tune Jas had taught her last night. Gina's cloud of yellow cotton-wool hair looked extra fluffy this afternoon and Becky thought she looked more like a ghost than ever, with her pale face and silvery eyes. She had a loud voice, which wouldn't have been bad if she'd managed to hit the right notes with it. As she sang she jumped around the stage as if someone had put itching powder down

52

her sweatshirt. There were giggles all round the gym and after just a few bars the band stopped.

'Oh dear!' said Emma, trying not to laugh. 'That wasn't very good at all.'

Liz took Becky by the hand and began leading her through the crowd, where Jas was lining up the girls waiting to sing. 'There you are!' Jas said excitedly. 'I've been looking for you everywhere. What took you so long?'

'I had to go and change,' Becky snapped. So much for her just being able to walk into the band, as Jas had promised. She began to feel really nervous.

Just then the next girl began to sing. She looked very glamorous, with long black hair, but she had a strange, rasping voice that didn't sound natural, and when she had to hit a high note her voice cracked. 'That's Kirsty, the lead guitarist's girlfriend.' Jas bristled. 'She's in the third year. Isn't she dreadful?' But even though Kirsty couldn't sing, the band kept playing right through to the end of the song.

The next few singers were no better and they were quickly cut off in mid-note. 'Your turn.' Jas gave Becky a thumbs-up sign as she took the microphone.

But Becky didn't need the encouragement. Though she was nervous, she was sure she could sing better than the others. Knowing that she looked the part helped, too.

The band began to play, but for some reason they were playing the song far too slowly. Becky stopped them.

'Could you play it a bit faster?' She tapped out the rhythm against the microphone stand. They looked at her in surprise, then the lead guitarist started at an even slower speed than before. Becky glowered but the band ignored her.

Something, she thought, *is going on here.* But it didn't matter. She started to sing in her natural, clear voice, dancing to the music at the same time. A few people in the gym began to dance too. But just as they were all beginning to enjoy themselves, the band stopped. There was a ripple of applause.

'Why did you stop?' Becky demanded. But the lead guitarist just turned his back on her. Becky felt angry. He hadn't helped her to do her best. If they'd played on, she could have had the whole gym dancing and clapping. Even so, she felt pleased with herself. She'd like to see someone else do better.

'They didn't give you a proper chance!' Jas fumed as Becky handed over the microphone to the next girl. 'Don't worry, though. It's in the bag. They've got to choose you.'

Just then a hand tapped Becky on the shoulder. She swung round expecting to see Liz or Charlie. But it was Daniel Armstrong.

'You were great, Becky.' He gave her one of his gorgeous smiles.

'Thanks, I enjoyed doing it.' Everyone was looking at them, but Becky didn't care.

'You know, when I saw you the other day I had a feeling that I'd seen you somewhere before.'

Becky was puzzled. 'I've only lived in Wetherton a week, so—'

He stopped her. 'No, I had a feeling I'd seen you on TV, maybe. And then watching you sing and dance just now, I'm certain I've seen you before.

Your hair was different, but your face looks familiar. It's your voice, too.'

The smile froze on Becky's face. For a second she couldn't breathe, and her heart began to pound. This was terrible! Daniel didn't know it, but he'd recognised her as the Kelly Kid. That had to be it. Becky swallowed nervously and laughed. 'Me, a TV star? Oh, sure!' And then she added cheekily, 'Is this a line you use on all the girls?'

'Hey, it's the truth!' he protested. 'Perhaps I've got it wrong, but I'm sure I recognise you.'

I'm sure you do, too, Becky said to herself. Oh, why had she got up and sung in front of everyone? How could she have been so stupid? It was just asking to be recognised. Why couldn't she just have kept a low profile instead of showing off? Now it would only be a matter of time before Daniel put two and two together and realised she was the Kelly Kid. 'I'm sure you haven't seen me on TV,' she said firmly. It wasn't exactly a lie. The Kelly Kid wasn't actually *her*, was it?

Daniel shrugged. He looked embarrassed. 'Forget it then. I must have made a mistake.' He glanced over her shoulder and said with relief, 'Anyway, it looks like the Porcupines are going to make their choice.' Instantly Becky forgot all about the Kelly Kid.

The band, including Jas, had gone into a huddle in the far corner of the gym. Becky could see them talking to one another. Jas was waving her hands about.

Liz came over to Becky. 'I'm sure they're going to pick you,' she said. 'You were the best, easily.'

But something was going on in the corner. There was a lot of head-shaking and Jas stamped her foot angrily. Then the band's drummer picked up the microphone. 'Thank you all for coming to the audition. It's been a difficult decision but we've decided that Kirsty Gregory is going to be the new backing singer with the band.'

'No!' Becky, Liz and several other people all gasped at once.

'I don't believe it. There's a mistake – there must be,' said Liz. 'Kirsty was the worst singer of all. Even Gina sounded better.'

But Becky knew in her heart there was no mistake . . .

'It was a fix!' Jas kicked one of the wooden benches in the girls' changing room, where Becky was getting back into uniform. 'They played too slowly to make it more difficult, and they stopped as soon as you really got going. They didn't want you to be too popular with the audience.'

'But Kirsty sounds so terrible. That's what I don't understand,' said Becky, pulling on her school shoes. 'Everyone'll just laugh when she sings.'

'It's got nothing to do with whether she can sing or not. She wanted to be in the band – especially when she heard that the Porcupines would be appearing with Rory Todd. So her boyfriend fixed it for her,' Jas explained. 'He said that if we didn't have Kirsty in the band he'd quit as lead guitarist. And what kind of band would it be without a lead guitar? So the others all agreed to take Kirsty on.'

Charlie gave a hollow laugh. 'When Rory Todd

hears her sing he'll forget all about including the Porcupines in the video.'

'That's what I told them,' agreed Jas. 'And they said that she'll sing quietly so no one can hear her.' There were gasps of disbelief.

'Anyway, Rory won't want you to actually play on his record, will he?' Liz added thoughtfully. 'He'll just get you to mime. So I suppose it doesn't really matter what the band sounds like.'

Becky blew her nose. She felt like crying, but she wasn't going to give anyone the satisfaction of seeing her in tears. 'That doesn't make me feel any better,' she said bitterly. 'I wouldn't have minded the chance of miming with Rory Todd. It's not fair.'

'No, it's not.' Even Charlie, who'd been so hostile to begin with, was on her side now. 'You were the best singer and you deserved that place in the band – so what can we do about it?'

All four of them looked at one another and shook their heads.

So was that it? thought Becky. Had her last chance of appearing with Rory Todd just vanished?

'Becky!' Susie shouted from the bottom of the stairs. 'It's your mum on the phone.'

'Mum?' Becky galloped down the stairs in her pyjamas. 'What's she doing, calling so late?' She'd been just about to go to bed.

'Oh, I've got the time lag muddled up again!' her mother said when Becky told her it was bedtime in Wetherton. 'Don't worry, darling, I can't talk to you for too long, so you won't lose your beauty sleep.'

'Mum, something really great's happened at school,'

Becky began. She wanted to tell her about Rory Todd's visit.

'Has it? That's nice. But I really wanted to tell you some good news of my own. I've been asked to go out to Los Angeles to discuss a role in a movie. Isn't that wonderful?'

'Yes, it is.' Becky was pleased for her mum.

'I thought I'd phone and let you know. And maybe during the next school holidays you could come over and visit. We could go to Disneyland. Would you like that?'

'Yes, that would be great,' Becky replied. Yet somehow she didn't feel quite as enthusiastic as expected. 'Mum, Rory Todd's coming to visit the school. He used to be a pupil there, like me.'

'Did he?' Her mother sounded distracted and Becky could hear someone else talking in the background. 'Look, Becky,' she said after a pause. 'I've got to go. Are you settling in with Dad all right?'

'Yeah. And when Rory Todd comes, he's going to make a video—'

'I'm sorry, Becky, but I really have to go. I'll call you in a few days. All right, darling?' And before Becky could say goodbye, she'd gone.

Becky hung up the phone and went to the fridge to get herself some milk. It was great to hear her mother's voice, but now Becky missed her all the more. And if her mother went to Los Angeles that would be even further away, on the other side of America. Becky spilled some milk on the blue-tiled kitchen counter and had to look for a cloth to mop it up.

Why did everything have to be so difficult? she

wondered. It was all so complicated. She'd love to go to see her mum and visit Disneyland, and yet there was something about the way her mother had talked which made Becky feel that she had other, more important things on her mind.

Then there was Rory Todd and the video. Becky pulled up a stool and perched at the counter while she drank her glass of milk. Why did everything keep going wrong? She'd been so certain of getting a place in the band, and it had been snatched away from her. It made her feel helpless, as if there was nothing she could do to meet her favourite pop star.

And then there was the Kelly Kid. What was Becky going to do if Jas gave away her secret, or Daniel Armstrong put two and two together? She'd have the whole school laughing at her. It would be unbearable – and yet there was nothing she could do to stop it happening. All she could do was hope. But deep down, she knew that wasn't enough.

'I can see your tonsils,' Becky said as Charlie yawned again. 'And they're not a pretty sight.'

'Sorry.' Charlie put her hand over her mouth. 'This Rory Todd thing is driving me crazy. I was lying in bed thinking about it till late. And even when I go to sleep I dream about him.'

'And you're complaining about that?' Liz arrived and put her school bag carefully on the desk. 'Last night I dreamt I was in detention with Mr Heyward and Kirsty Gregory. She kept singing all the time and he wouldn't let me out!'

'Oh, no,' moaned Charlie, rearranging the scarves

around her neck. 'I'd forgotten we've got a detention this afternoon.'

Becky wished she could forget about it. She hadn't dreamt about Kirsty, but she had lain awake for hours the previous night thinking about all her problems. In the end she'd decided that what she really needed was a miracle – and miracles seemed a bit thin on the ground at Bell Street at the moment.

Miss Tyler came bustling in with a pile of handouts. 'Pass these round, please.' She gave them to Jamie Thompson, who started distributing them.

'Anything exciting?' Becky asked Liz, who had grabbed one first.

'It's a school trip – an adventure weekend in Wales.' Liz's face lit up. 'Sounds fantastic. Pony trekking, canoeing, abseiling . . . '

'Great! I'll go,' Charlie said, stifling another yawn. 'If I survive all this Rory Todd mania, that is.'

'Everyone'll go, won't they?' asked Becky. 'It'll be fun.'

'Well, it's expensive. And,' Liz gestured with her head towards Emma, 'there are one or two people who might not enjoy it,' she said softly.

Becky didn't understand. 'Emma? Why not?'

'Because of her leg,' Liz whispered.

'What about her leg?' Becky asked, puzzled.

'She's got a limp. Hadn't you noticed?' Liz sounded cross.

'Are you sure? She seems okay to me.' Becky tried to think of how Emma had walked the other day. She'd walked slightly strangely, perhaps – but only as if her shoe was rubbing.

Liz looked confused. 'She was born with a bad leg. I can remember when we were at junior school together she was always going into hospital for operations. She's always had a bad limp.'

Becky raised her eyebrows. 'So that's why you were fussing round her like a mother hen the other day when she fell over!'

'Yes,' Liz said indignantly. 'She could have been badly hurt. She's not very strong.'

Becky looked over at Emma. She seemed perfectly strong and healthy. 'I can't see anything wrong with her,' she muttered to Liz. 'Maybe all the operations have made her better.'

Liz pursed her lips. She looked uncertain, as if it was a long time since she'd stopped to look at Emma properly. 'Well . . . '

Charlie had been listening. 'I don't know about Emma, but Jamie Thompson doesn't look too thrilled about the adventure weekend.'

'What's wrong with *him*?' Becky asked sarcastically. 'Has he got an invisible bad leg too?'

Charlie snorted with laughter. 'No, idiot! He's just never really fitted in, has he, Liz? He came to this school two terms ago but I don't think he's made many friends.'

'He doesn't say much.' Becky looked over at Jamie. She'd never taken much notice of him before. He seemed nice enough, but he always had his head in a book. In a way, he was like Emma; he didn't make much of an impact.

Miss Tyler interrupted Becky's thoughts. 'Put those handouts away safely and give them to your parents when you go home after school,' she said breezily.

'Now, we still need ideas for our stall for the summer fête. Have you come up with anything?'

Today there was a sea of hands and suggestions: hoop-la, a hat stall, bric-a-brac . . .

'I could bring my pony, Jasper, and give pony rides,' Gina Galloway suggested with a smug smile and a shake of her fluffy yellow hair.

'Trust Gina to have her own pony,' growled Liz. 'Just because her parents are rich enough to give her anything she wants.'

'That sounds a good idea.' Miss Tyler was interested, but before she could say anything more there were protests from the back of the class.

'Miss, Gina told us that her pony bites!'

'And that he's so wild, she's the only one who can ride him.'

'Ah.' Miss Tyler raised her eyebrows. 'In that case perhaps it's not such a good idea after all – though thank you for offering, Gina.'

Gina blushed, clearly embarrassed.

Good, Becky said to herself. *That'll teach her to boast.*

Miss Tyler took out a list. 'These are the stalls that the other classes are running. There's already a bric-a-brac stall and a hat stall. What we need is something truly original – something that no one will be able to resist spending their money on.'

'At this rate we'll be the only class without a stall,' muttered Liz.

But Becky wasn't listening. *Maybe I don't need a miracle after all*, she said to herself. *Maybe a good idea will be enough.* That was it! If she could just come up with a brilliant idea for a stall at the fête, Miss Tyler would have to choose her as one of the people to appear in Rory's video. All Becky needed now was one solid gold idea. She shut her eyes and waited for inspiration.

'What's wrong?' Liz interrupted. 'Have you got a headache?'

Becky opened her eyes and sighed. Perhaps this wasn't going to be quite as easy as she'd thought . . .

6

The first lesson of the day was art. Becky was relieved, because it was the kind of lesson which gave her plenty of time to think. They were working on collages. The teacher had offered them four themes to choose from – earth, air, fire and water. Becky chose water and started by covering her sheet of paper in shades of blue and green paint. Then she began sorting through some old magazines from the resources cupboard, looking for pictures of fish and underwater creatures. Next to her, Emma was working quietly on her 'Air' collage.

On the other side of the room there were giggles as Charlie and Ryan and some of the others looked through magazines and chose images to cut out. Suddenly Becky felt the hairs on the back of her neck stand on end.

'I am the Kelly Kid and I love Kelly's Krunch!' Ryan was singing in a silly high-pitched voice. Becky didn't dare turn round to see what was happening. She froze with her head down over her collage so that no one would see her reaction. Why wasn't the teacher telling him to be quiet? But she didn't seem to be around.

Then things got worse. 'I'm the Kelly Kid,' someone else sang. It sounded suspiciously like Gina Galloway's snide voice.

'Oh, shut up, Kelly! I hate that cereal,' called a voice from across the room. There was loud laughter. Emma looked over, then turned to Becky.

'Ryan's found a picture of the Kelly Kid – the one in the advert. Do you remember her from TV? The one with the ginger plaits and goofy grin?'

Becky nodded, white-faced.

Emma was watching what was happening. 'Good, Charlie's grabbed the magazine from Ryan. Maybe he'll shut up now.'

Becky felt a surge of relief. She could start to breathe again.

But before she could relax, she heard Charlie's low chuckle. 'Hey, Becky, you know what? There's something about this Kelly Kid that reminds me of you!'

Becky gulped. She turned round slowly with a feeling of dread.

'Sit down, Charlie, and finish your collage,' Jas called. But Charlie wasn't listening. She walked over to Becky's table.

'Look at this photo, Becky. It's weird. You've got to admit she does look like you. She's got the same sort of smile. She's even got a crooked little tooth like you.' Charlie pointed to the photograph. Becky pretended to look and kept her lips firmly closed. Her face was going red, she knew, and there was nothing she could do to stop it.

'She's nothing like me,' she protested. But then Charlie looked her full in the eye.

'Becky? Are you all right? You're looking very guilty.' Charlie put her head on one side and peered through her glasses in that strange way she sometimes did. 'It *is* you, isn't it?'

Becky couldn't deny it.

Emma leaned over her shoulder and had a look, too. 'What's this? You're the Kelly Kid? Why didn't you tell us, Becky?'

'You *are* the Kelly Kid!' Charlie's voice was so loud, everyone in the room heard it. She began to howl with laughter. 'No wonder you're so embarrassed!'

'Kelly! Kelly! Kelly!' chanted some kids at another table. Everyone in the room burst out laughing.

Becky buried her face in her hands. It was all starting again, just as it had at her last school.

'The Kelly Kid makes me sick,' someone shouted and made a gagging sound. Becky felt utterly humiliated. Was she never going to live this down? Two hands fell on her shoulders.

'Becky, are you okay?' It was Jas. 'I didn't tell anyone – promise. Charlie figured it out all on her own.'

Charlie was surprised. 'You mean you knew all the time? Why didn't you tell us that Becky was the Kelly Kid?'

'Because Becky wanted to keep it a secret.' Jas's eyes glittered with irritation. 'Honestly, Charlie, sometimes you're so insensitive.'

Charlie must have felt bad because she said sympathetically, 'I didn't mean to upset you, Becky. I didn't realise you were so touchy about it. It's just that the Kelly Kid's such a joke.'

'I know!' Becky cried. 'And ever since I made that stupid advert people have been laughing at me. Just listen to them now.'

Her secret was out – and soon everyone in the school would know that she was the ridiculous Kelly Kid . . .

'At first I didn't understand why you wanted to keep it a secret. Get lost!' Liz snapped at a first-year who was humming the Kelly Kid song loudly as he passed the lunch queue, where she and Becky were standing. 'I'd have been proud to have appeared in an advert. But maybe being famous isn't always fun.'

Becky tried to ignore all the attention, but it was difficult. Everyone seemed to have something to say about the Kelly Kid. And usually what they had to say was nasty.

'Was it like this at your last school?' Charlie glared at a boy who'd stuck out his tongue at Becky.

'No, it was worse,' Becky said emphatically. 'It started like this. Then they began telling Kelly Kid jokes, like "Why do people always look twice at the Kelly Kid?" '

'I don't know, why?' supplied Jas.

' "Because the first time they can't believe their eyes." '

'That's not so bad,' Liz said, giggling. 'You can just laugh that off.'

Becky bit her lip. 'It's not so easy. Anyway, that wasn't the end of it. Some of the older kids started bullying me. They said I must have made a lot of money from the adverts, and they wanted it.'

'Oh, Becky!' Liz looked really concerned. 'That's terrible. I didn't realise. Now I understand why you wanted to keep it a secret.'

Jas patted her on the shoulder. 'You don't have to worry about any of that happening here, Becky. We won't let it.'

That made Becky feel a little better, but even so,

she was still afraid. And even if she didn't get bullied, she was going to have to put up with everyone making fun of her.

'Still, it could be worse,' Liz said optimistically.

'How?' Becky demanded.

'You could have appeared on TV as that tomato in the sauce advert. Now that would be *really* embarrassing.'

'Or as the green fluffy monster in that programme for little kids – you know, *Moonshine*,' added Charlie, playing with one of her scarves.

'If I was dressed as a tomato or a green monster no one would be able to recognise me,' Becky pointed out.

'I suppose not,' said Liz. 'How did you get into the advert in the first place?' she asked.

'Through my mum,' Becky said through gritted teeth. 'She heard that they were looking for a girl to appear in it, so I went along to the audition. I thought it would be fun.'

Jas raised her eyebrows. 'Didn't they tell you the Kelly Kid was supposed to be so awful?'

'No.' Becky shook her head, remembering the shock when she'd first seen the outfit and wig they wanted her to wear. 'They didn't explain it. And they didn't explain about the trap-door, either,' she added bitterly. She could still remember the humiliation she'd felt when she saw the whole advertisement for the first time. It showed her tap-dancing across the stage and singing the Kelly's Krunch song in a silly voice. Suddenly a trap-door opened up and she fell through it. And a man's voice said, *'We're sorry about that, it was in very bad taste. But Kelly's Krunch is a very good taste, we promise.'*

Liz and Jas couldn't hide their giggles at the mention of the trap-door. 'I used to think it was really funny when the Kelly Kid fell through the floor,' said Jas.

'Hilarious!' Becky responded sarcastically, but she didn't say more because across the dining hall she'd spotted a tall, dark-haired figure. It was Daniel Armstrong and he was watching her closely. Becky's heart gave a leap. Daniel was so good-looking – and so nice, too. She gave him the best smile she could manage.

For a moment he seemed to smile back at her. Then a girl who'd been standing nearby went up to him and whispered something in his ear. Daniel looked at Becky again – and this time she saw him burst out laughing.

Becky turned away. She didn't want to see any more. Daniel Armstrong had laughed when he found out that she was the Kelly Kid – just like everyone else. And to think she'd thought he was nice!

On Saturday morning Becky took her mail down the garden to read. It was a clear, sunny day, and she perched on the swing under the old apple tree and read the letters that had come from two of her friends in London. They were full of gossip and stories about people she knew from her old school – who was going out with whom, who'd had a fight, who was in trouble with the teachers. Oh, it would be good to be back there, Becky thought, clutching the letters and gazing at the cloudless blue sky. Maybe she'd had some hard times, but at least she'd felt she belonged there. At Bell Street she felt like an outsider. And now they knew about the Kelly Kid, how was she ever going to fit in?

And at least in London there had been things to do over the weekend. Wetherton was so much quieter. Although it was prettier, with more trees and space between the houses, the shopping centre wasn't very big, and there was only one cinema. It couldn't compare to the excitement of London.

'Here you are!' Mr Burns came strolling down the garden. 'Have you got anything planned today?'

Becky shook her head grimly. That was a joke! Liz and Jas had just waved goodbye after school yesterday without a word.

Mr Burns leaned against the apple tree. 'Susie and I were wondering about taking a look at the leisure centre. It's just a couple of miles out of town. Someone was saying there's an ice-rink and a swimming pool. We could go for a swim.'

'No, you two go if you want.' Becky pushed off the ground with her baseball boots and began to swing.

'Too embarrassed to be seen out with your wrinkly old dad, eh?'

Even that couldn't make Becky smile. Although his hair was beginning to get a bit thin on top and he did have a few wrinkles round his eyes, Mr Burns was still quite young and good looking. Becky just went on swinging.

'Are you still angry with Susie?' he asked. 'I thought you two had made up.'

'We have,' Becky said, annoyed.

'Then what's the problem?'

At last she couldn't keep it to herself any more. 'I hate this place!' she shouted. 'I want to go back to London. And I'm not going to the stupid leisure centre in case we meet some of the kids from school. They found out about the Kelly Kid – even though you said they'd never guess!' She delivered the last few words with a hostile glare.

'Tell me what happened,' Mr Burns said calmly. So she did – all about the art class and the trouble since then.

'Give it a couple of days. Something else will happen and they'll forget,' consoled Mr Burns.

'No they won't.' Becky was determined. 'I don't want to go back to school. I haven't got any friends there. All my friends are in London. Everyone at Bell Street is laughing at me.'

Mr Burns was silent for a moment, then said, 'It doesn't help if you take it so seriously. You have to admit the Kelly Kid is kind of funny.'

'Funny? Ha!' Becky snapped. 'You don't know what it's like to have people treating you as if you're a joke!' she said accusingly.

'Yes I do.' Her father pulled a pained face. 'My first couple of days teaching at the college were terrible. Everything I did went wrong.'

Becky tried to pretend she wasn't interested. But curiosity got the better of her. 'What happened?'

'Well, when I got to the college on the first day I mistook the caretaker for the principal. And then I broke the photocopier by pressing the wrong buttons. But the worst was when I gave my first lecture.'

He went bright red! 'What did you do?'

'Everything was going fine. At the end of class I turned to leave the lecture room and there were two doors behind me. I couldn't remember which one was the way out, so I walked through the one on the right-hand side – straight into the storeroom where they keep the slide projector and the other equipment.'

Becky couldn't help giggling. 'It must have been embarrassing to come out again and try the other door with everyone watching.'

'It was far worse than that!' exclaimed Mr Burns. 'I felt a complete fool, so I thought I'd stay there until all the students had gone, then sneak out.'

'So what happened?'

'I waited five minutes until I thought everyone had left the lecture room, then I opened the storeroom door and came out – and they were still sitting there, waiting to see what I was doing. They all thought it was hysterically funny! I've never felt so embarrassed in my life.'

'I know the feeling,' Becky said with a nod. 'It's awful. And there's nothing you can do about it.'

'Yes there is,' countered Mr Burns. 'Instead of getting angry, I laughed about it too. And now, whenever I finish a lecture, I make a joke about getting out of the room. Sometimes I ask one of the students to show me the way, sometimes I deliberately open the wrong door and pretend to walk into the storeroom again.'

Becky wasn't convinced. 'I don't see how that helps. After all, they're still laughing at you, aren't they?'

'It's different. If people see you're really embarrassed, they'll keep laughing at you and making you feel bad. But if you turn the whole thing into a joke against yourself, they'll get bored with it. At least now everyone in the college knows who I am, and they know I've got a sense of humour. Instead of being a total disaster, my mistake helped break the ice.'

Becky sighed. 'And how is this supposed to make me feel better about the Kelly Kid?'

Mr Burns shrugged. 'Maybe you can learn to laugh about the Kelly Kid instead of letting it bug you. Think about the good things. At least everybody at Bell Street School knows who you are now.'

'Great,' Becky said without enthusiasm. 'Everyone knows I was on TV making a fool of myself.'

'There has to be a way of turning the Kelly Kid to your advantage,' Mr Burns persisted.

'I don't see how.' How could she change the fact that everyone hated the Kelly Kid and loved to laugh at Becky Burns?

Mr Burns shrugged and put his hands in his pockets. 'Think about it.' He glanced at the letters she was still clutching in her hand. 'And why don't you also think about inviting a couple of your friends to come up for a weekend or in the holidays? It'll make a change from London for them. It only takes an hour and a half on the train.'

'Do you really mean it?' Becky said excitedly.

'Of course!' Mr Burns laughed. 'You can't go back to your old life in London – but maybe we can bring a bit of it here for you.'

'But there's nothing to *do* in Wetherton.' Becky wrinkled her nose.

'You could go riding,' Mr Burns suggested. 'I pass a riding stable on my way to college every morning.'

Becky was interested; she'd never been riding in London!

'And there's the leisure centre, of course.' Mr Burns grinned. 'Why don't you come and check it out now, so you can take them there yourself?'

'Well . . . ' But no matter how hard Becky tried to keep up her bad mood, she couldn't prevent herself feeling more enthusiastic. Maybe her problems weren't quite so bad after all.

She jumped down from the swing. 'I suppose I'd better go and get my swimsuit.'

And halfway up the garden path she had an idea. A *brilliant* idea.

7

'Hi, Jamie!' Becky called cheerfully as she passed Jamie Thompson in the playground on Monday morning. He looked round in surprise, but he didn't say anything.

Hmm . . . I was only trying to be friendly, Becky said to herself. But she wasn't going to let Jamie spoil her good mood. The others were sitting in their usual spot on the grass bank.

'I see you're chatting up Jamie Thompson now,' joked Liz. 'As if Daniel Armstrong isn't enough for you!'

'All I did was say hello,' Becky replied, testing the grass to make sure it wasn't damp before she sat down. 'He didn't even say hello back.'

'He's a bit strange,' Charlie muttered. She was trying to plait her hair and was getting it into a tangle. 'He hardly ever talks to anyone except Emma – and she thinks he's a bit of a wimp.'

'He's not bad-looking,' Jas defended. 'He was wearing a really great shirt the other day. It must have cost a fortune.' She was searching around in the bottom of her backpack.

'What are you looking for?' Becky asked. 'Lost your gum?'

'My cheque and application form for the adventure

weekend,' Jas said anxiously. 'Maybe I left them at home. I hope so, or my mum'll go spare! What about you, Becky?' Jas asked, stuffing everything back into her bag. In went a school sweatshirt, lunch box, gym kit, towel, hairbrush, magazines, exercise books, a pencil case, a carton of juice, two packets of chewing-gum, a tiny brown teddy bear, a Rory Todd cassette . . .

'I'm coming, sure, but I forgot to talk to my parents about it over the weekend. I had other things on my mind.' *Like all my problems*, Becky said to herself as she watched Jas. How could she get so much in one bag?

Liz was quiet. 'You're going to come, aren't you?' Becky asked.

Liz gave a wistful smile. 'Well, my parents said I'll have to wait and see about the money. They say there are more important things to spend money on, like new shoes.' She held one foot up. 'This is my only decent pair at the moment, and I've almost grown out of them.'

'It wouldn't be the same if we have to go without you,' Charlie said sadly. She looked up just as Emma Pennington walked past. 'How about you, Emma? Are you going on the adventure trip?'

'I want to go,' Emma said emphatically, 'but . . . We'll see.' She looked worried.

Liz smiled grimly. 'Same here. Maybe you and I will have to stay at home while all the lucky ones go off.'

'Not if I can help it,' Emma said sharply. 'I've had enough of staying at home while everyone else has a good time.' For a second she looked amazed, as if

78

she could hardly believe what she'd said. Then she walked away.

Liz watched disbelievingly. 'What's happened to Emma?' she asked. 'She's not normally like that.'

Becky, too, couldn't help wondering what accounted for the change in Emma. Something told her they hadn't heard the last about Emma and the adventure weekend.

Miss Tyler was looking more subdued than usual. This morning she was wearing a dark green dress and the only hint of red about her was her red earrings. She seemed quieter, too.

'Miss, when are you going to choose the people for Rory Todd's video?' asked Ryan after the register had been called.

For a moment Miss Tyler looked puzzled, as if she'd forgotten all about Rory Todd. Then she remembered. 'Next Monday – so you'd all better be on your best behaviour until then.' There was a loud groan from the class.

Miss Tyler held up her hand. 'We don't have time to talk about that. This morning we've got to decide on the stall we're going to run at the fête on Saturday. We should have made up our minds by now. Does anyone have a new idea?'

Becky's hand shot up. Miss Tyler nodded. 'Go ahead, Becky.'

'It's a good idea but it needs to be kept a secret,' Becky explained. 'Can I come and tell you about it?'

Miss Tyler was surprised. 'Okay! It certainly sounds unusual!'

Becky went up to the teacher's table. She was feeling a bit anxious. If Miss Tyler liked the idea, it could be the answer to everyone's problems, including her own. If not, she'd have to start thinking all over again. She bent her head and began to explain her plans in a low voice.

After a while Miss Tyler began to smile. 'Yes,' she said as she wrote something down on a notepad. 'Yes, I think that could work. I'll arrange to have the stall prepared for you.'

Becky returned to her seat looking pleased with herself. 'Hey, Kelly, what's the big secret?' Ryan Bryson called from the back of the class, but Becky just ignored him.

'Becky has had a wonderful idea,' announced Miss Tyler. 'She and I will be keeping it under wraps until the day of the fête – but I think I can safely say no one else will have a stall like it.'

'What *is* it?' whispered Liz, but Becky just shook her head.

'If I tell you, it would ruin the surprise,' she said simply.

'What do we have to do?' asked Charlie.

Miss Tyler smiled. 'There's no hard work involved. All we need are some plastic buckets and sponges. Can I have some volunteers to bring those on the day of the fête?' Most of the class put their hands up.

'And everybody should wear old clothes,' added Becky.

Liz gave Becky a sideways look. 'Becky Burns, what are you up to now?'

Becky just smiled.

'I promise to keep it a secret,' Liz vowed as the girls sat working in the library. 'Come on, tell me or it'll drive me crazy with curiosity!'

'I can't take the risk.' Becky pulled out a book from one of the shelves. 'Sorry, Liz, it's nothing personal. But my idea will work best if it's a big surprise on the day.'

'Well, I hope it makes a lot of money,' Liz snapped as she took a neatly sharpened pencil out of her case. Liz's pencils always seemed to be sharp. And Liz's pencil case was never full of old bits of eraser and broken pens, like everyone else's. Everything was just perfect!

'It will make lots of money.' Becky crossed her fingers. *It better had,* she said to herself. All her hopes were pinned on a big success.

They were interrupted by Ryan Bryson, who popped his head round the bookcase. 'I know what your secret is, Kelly.'

'No, you don't,' Becky challenged him. 'And my name's not Kelly.'

Liz had overheard and almost jumped on Ryan. 'What is it?' she insisted. 'Come on, Ryan, tell me.'

'It's a car wash, of course.' He looked at Becky knowingly. 'I'm right, aren't I? That's why you wanted us to bring buckets and sponges and wear our old clothes. You're going to make us clean people's cars.'

'A car wash? Is that all?' Liz looked disappointed. 'I thought it would be something more exciting.'

'Actually it's a very good idea,' mused Charlie, who'd been looking through an atlas and checking her geography homework. She shook her plait back over her shoulder. 'If we washed a hundred cars and charged people a pound each we'd raise a hundred pounds for charity.'

Ryan rolled his eyes in horror! 'A *hundred* cars? That's slave labour! It'd kill us.'

But it wasn't hard work that Liz was worrying about. 'If it's a car wash, shouldn't we advertise so that people know they should bring their cars to the fête? How are we going to make money if they walk? You've got to organise these things properly, Becky.'

'If you want anything organised, Liz is your girl,' Charlie commented snidely.

'It is going to be a car wash, isn't it?' demanded Ryan.

'So shall I make some posters?' asked Liz.

But Becky wouldn't say a word.

Charlie groaned as she collapsed on the changing-room bench. 'I'm exhausted!' she complained.

Becky laughed. 'Poor old Charlie! You need to get fit. I've got an exercise video at home. That'll soon give you some muscles.'

'I don't want to develop muscles,' Charlie protested, sitting up slowly and taking off her trainers. 'And I don't want to run ten times round the track, either! Why won't the gym teacher just leave us alone?'

Liz and Jas came jogging in, pink-cheeked. 'It's good for you,' Liz said, out of breath. 'At least, that's what they keep saying when we try to stop.'

'I'm not complaining,' said Jas. 'I prefer running and exercise to doing maths and French.' Jas was a good athlete – Becky had noticed that. She was the fastest runner in the class.

Becky looked round the changing room. All the girls from 2K were there except for one. 'Where's Emma?' she asked. 'She was in class earlier this afternoon.'

'Emma doesn't do gym,' Jas said quickly.

'It's her leg,' added Liz. 'I told you she had problems with it. She goes and helps in the library while we're here.'

Becky shrugged. As far as Liz was concerned, Emma was quite seriously disabled. But from what Becky had seen, that was far from the truth. But she wasn't going to argue. She reached for the yellow towel sticking out of her bag and gave it a sharp tug.

Liz shrieked and jumped back. 'What's that?' she yelled as a shower of brown flakes shot up in the air and fell all over the floor. There were shouts from across the room.

'Oh, no!' Becky cried as she picked up her bag. 'I don't believe it!'

'What is it?' Liz picked some of the flakes out of her hair. 'What's happened?'

Becky clenched her fists. 'Someone's filled my bag with Kelly's Krunch! And my shoes! I don't believe it.'

'What a mess!' Liz exclaimed, looking around.

'It doesn't taste bad,' Charlie said, popping some of the cereal into her mouth.

But Becky wasn't amused. 'I suppose this is someone's idea of a joke! We'd better get a broom and clear it up.'

Jas frowned. 'I thought you were exaggerating when you said people at your old school played tricks on you. But not after this! Who could have done it?'

Gina Galloway's fluffy blond head turned to stare. Then she looked away and sniggered loudly.

'I'm not going to waste my time trying to find out,' Becky decided aloud. She was furious. There were bits of cereal everywhere – in her purse, her folders, her clothes . . .

'We'll give you a hand.' Charlie scrunched across the floor to find a dustpan. They had to clear up the mess in a hurry – their next lesson began in just a few minutes.

'You're being very cool about this, Becky,' Jas observed, rubbing her hair dry after her shower. 'If I were you, I'd be going crazy!'

Becky ground her teeth and pulled on her skirt. Though she'd tipped the cereal out of her shoes, her toes still felt gritty. 'The more furious I get, the more satisfaction it'll give to whoever did this. And anyway, I think I've found an answer to the problem.'

It had better be the solution, Becky thought grimly to herself. Because if her plan didn't work, she was really going to be in trouble!

8

'Testing, testing, testing ... one, two, three ... ' Mr Heyward's voice blared from loudspeakers in the trees around the playing field, where dozens of stalls had been set out for the fête. Bunting and balloons dangled from the branches. Though the fête wasn't yet open, there were already crowds of parents and pupils milling around, inspecting the things for sale and checking up on the events for the afternoon. Only one person didn't seem to be enjoying it, and that was Liz.

'I can't believe it!' she said worriedly. 'We're all here with our buckets and sponges, and Becky's not even going to turn up! I told her she should let me organise things properly.'

'Calm down, Liz.' Jas was dressed in an old black T-shirt covered with paint spatters and an ancient pair of jeans. She had dark glasses, too, which made her look very trendy. 'You know Becky's not like that. She'll be here.' She held out the programme of events. 'Have you seen this? There's a fashion show by the fifth-formers in the hall at two o'clock. I want to go to that.'

'And some of the other stalls are great,' Charlie declared as she arrived carrying a bucket. She looked very exotic in patchwork trousers and with long, dangly earrings and bracelets that jangled as she walked. '2C have made a gypsy tent in the drama studio. It's supposed to be really dark and spooky. Some of them are dressing up and telling fortunes. I think I'll go along later.'

Liz gave her a disapproving glance. 'It's only Lisa Willis with a teatowel round her head, so don't take it too seriously.'

'Isn't there anything you want to do?' asked Charlie.

'I'd like to have a look at 4F's pottery stall,' Liz admitted. 'They've been making things for weeks. And 5K are selling jewellery.'

'Well don't waste your money on the coconut shy,' advised Emma, joining them. She, too, was carrying a bucket. 'I've just seen Nicky Ashe sticking the coconuts in place with super-glue!' She turned to look at the low platform covered in plastic sheeting. 'Is this our stall?'

'Yes!' Liz raised her eyebrows. 'And no, I don't know what we're doing. You'll just have to ask Becky – if she ever turns up.'

'We could always sell the buckets if she doesn't come,' joked Jas. 'Hey, who's that?'

Coming towards them across the grass was a strange figure wearing a huge overcoat and a scarf around its head and face. It was carrying something rolled under its arm – and behind it walked a man and a woman, carrying two long poles.

'Becky?' Jas raised her sunglasses to take a better look.

'Sorry we're late. I was having trouble with my hair.' Becky handed over the bundle she had been carrying to Charlie and Emma. 'This is a banner. Can you two put it up over the platform?'

They unfolded it. 'You'll need these,' said Susie, helping them attach it to the two poles, which they stuck in the ground on either side of the platform.

' "THE KELLY KID – THE KID YOU LOVE TO HATE",' Jas read as the banner went up.

'Who made it?' asked Charlie. 'It's great!'

'Me and Susie.' Becky grinned. 'I'll just take off my coat and scarf.'

The others stood back in disbelief. Becky was dressed exactly like the Kelly Kid! She wore a red and white checked dress and a ginger wig with braids, and had given herself bright red cheeks and freckles.

'That's a truly disgusting dress,' Charlie muttered.

'Look at your face!' Ryan couldn't stop laughing.

Liz was puzzled. 'Okay, so you're the Kelly Kid, but now what are we going to do?'

'Fill those buckets with water,' instructed Becky. 'Make it warm water, please. And when my dad's got the sound system going, I'm going to get up on the platform and sing and dance to the Kelly Kid tune.'

Jas began to laugh as she figured out Becky's plan. 'And we're going to ask people to pay to throw a wet sponge at the Kelly Kid! Becky, it's a brilliant idea!'

'I told you so, didn't I?' Becky gave a little curtsy. 'Now you'd better get that water fast. The fête is about to begin!'

'I am the Kelly Kid, and I love Kelly's Krunch.' Before she could get any further with the song, a wet sponge hit Becky in the face. There was a huge cheer from the crowd round the stand.

'Great shot!' yelled Ryan, scampering round the back of the platform to find the sponge.

Becky just kept smiling and singing in the lispy little-girl voice she'd used in the advert. *'Crunchy! Munchy! Kelly's Krunch is scrunchy! Eat it in the morning, eat it late at night—'* Another sponge whistled past her ear.

As the music changed Becky started to dance the silly tap-dance. Dripping sponges landed around her feet, but she just kicked them out of the way. The other kids in the class ran round picking them up and dunking them back in the buckets before selling them to the next customer. It didn't take long before everyone was soaked, but no one minded.

'This is the best stall at the fête!' Emma said excitedly as she collected the money from the people waiting in line. 'Look at poor Becky, she's dripping!'

But Becky didn't mind getting wet. And for once in her life, she didn't mind being the Kelly Kid, either. In fact she did all she could to be even more sickly and disgusting than she had been on the TV advert. And the more awful her smile and voice were, the more people loved it.

After she'd sung the Kelly Kid song a few times, Mr Burns put on a new tape and Becky sang some pop songs in the same terrible voice.

Jas watched in amazement. 'I can't believe this is the same Becky who sang for the Porcupines!' she said, giggling. 'Though even now she's better than Kirsty Gregory.'

'Get off! You're awful!' the crowd yelled. There weren't enough sponges to go around, so many people wanted to throw one.

After half an hour of singing and dancing, Becky decided to take a break. 'That's all for now, folks,' she announced. 'But I'll be back with more wonderful entertainment later.' There was a round of applause as she got down from the stage. Susie held out a big towel for her to dry off with.

Jas came over carrying a can of cola and a chocolate chip cookie. 'You could probably do with this,' she offered.

But before Becky could take so much as a bite, a crowd of kids gathered round. 'Can we have your autograph, Kelly?' one of them asked.

'You really want the Kelly Kid's autograph?' She couldn't believe it. Just yesterday they'd all been making fun of her. Now today they wanted her signature!

'Autographs are 50p,' Emma said firmly. 'All the money goes to charity.'

So this, Becky thought as she began signing autograph books, *is what it's like to be famous!*

'Hundred and forty-two, hundred and forty-three . . . ' Liz was adding up the piles of coins they'd brought back to the classroom.

'How did we do?' Becky asked as she returned from the changing rooms. She'd swapped the Kelly Kid's soaked dress for her own jeans and fitted white blouse. Her hair was damp, despite the wig she'd been wearing.

'Shhh, don't distract me!' Liz hissed, scribbling down figures on her clipboard.

'This is the third time she and Emma have tried adding it up,' explained Charlie, her bracelets clattering as she walked around. 'They keep getting a different total.'

Becky sat on the edge of the desk and waited for the result.

Just then Jas breezed in, wearing an amazing black hat with a huge red rose that she'd bought at the fête. 'Miss Tyler's coming to collect the dosh in a minute, so you two had better get your act together,' she warned. 'And I've had a brilliant idea. Why don't we go into town and have a pizza to celebrate? We all worked really hard this afternoon, so we deserve a treat.'

'That sounds great,' agreed Becky. 'I'll just have to go home and tell my dad and Susie.'

Liz finished her adding up. 'I'm not sure I can afford it,' she murmured. 'I'm trying to save up for the adventure weekend, remember?'

Becky waved her hand dismissively. 'Don't worry about that, Liz. I'll shout you.'

'No you won't!' Liz said proudly. 'I always pay my own way, Becky.'

'I'm sorry. I didn't mean to offend you,' Becky apologised. 'It's just that I'd really like you to come with us, Liz. It wouldn't be the same without you. And my mum sent me some money from America and told me to use it for a special occasion.'

'That's some mum you've got,' Jas said, sighing. 'Has she invited you over there to visit yet?'

Becky felt uncomfortable. She didn't want anyone to think she was boasting. 'She's said there might be a chance of my visiting her when she goes to California – but no promises.'

'You lucky thing!' Jas exclaimed.

Liz interrupted the conversation. 'Do you want to know the total before Miss Tyler runs off with the money?'

'Of course!' Jas made a sound like a fanfare of trumpets. 'Let's have it.'

'We made a total of one hundred and fifty-eight pounds and twenty pence!'

Charlie whistled in amazement. 'Are you sure? That's more than twice as much as we made last year!'

'And more than any other stall raised today,' Miss Tyler said from the doorway. She looked very dashing today in bright red trousers and overshirt. 'Congratulations to all of you. Without you and the Kelly Kid, Becky, we would have come nowhere in the money-raising league.' She glanced round and spotted Charlie's frown. 'Why are you looking so gloomy, Charlotte?'

Charlie raised her eyebrows. 'Because next year we'll have to beat our own record!'

Miss Tyler laughed as she took the money from Liz. 'Well, maybe Becky will come up with an even better idea for next year. Meanwhile, the cash has to go to the bank. See you all on Monday.'

'It was a great idea,' said Liz, patting Becky on the back when Miss Tyler had gone. 'Much better than a car wash. Now I understand why you wanted to keep it a secret. And nobody's ever going to make fun about you being the Kelly Kid after this!'

'That was part of my plan,' Becky admitted.

There was a twinkle in Jas's eye. 'And I think I know what the other part of the plan is!'

Becky fluttered her eyelashes innocently. 'I just

wanted 2K to have a good stall for the fête.'

'And make a record amount of money for charity,' observed Emma.

'And get chosen by Miss Tyler to be in the Rory Todd video?' Jas suggested.

Becky shrugged, but it was difficult to hide her pleasure. 'Maybe I did have that in mind, too.'

'And I wouldn't be surprised,' said Jas, 'if your plan has worked.'

As she walked up Church Street, Becky felt great. All her troubles had been solved in a single afternoon! The Kelly Kid wouldn't be giving her any problems from now on. Miss Tyler was bound to pick her to be in the video with Rory Todd. And now she was off to meet her friends and go for a pizza. What more could she ask for?

She slowed down to cross the road. A cyclist was heading in her direction, so she waited – and realised too late that it was Daniel Armstrong, riding straight towards her on his mountain bike.

'Hey, Becky!' He braked and stopped right in front of her. Becky wasn't sure what to do. If he was going to make fun of her, she didn't want to wait around and hear it. 'I've been meaning to talk to you for days.'

Becky couldn't stop herself blushing. She still felt angry with him for the way he'd laughed at her that lunchtime. Even so, he still looked really good in his faded jeans and baseball shirt. And his hazel eyes were still lovely.

'Really?' she asked making it sound as if she couldn't care less.

'That was a great idea for the fête this afternoon,' he began. A puzzled look crossed his face. 'Look, there's something I don't understand. Why didn't you tell me you were the Kelly Kid when I told you I thought I'd seen you on TV? Why was it such a big secret?'

Becky bit her lip. Surely the answer was obvious. 'Because I thought you'd just laugh at me.'

'Why should I laugh?'

'Because the Kelly Kid was such a big joke.' It was strange, but after what she'd done that afternoon, Becky didn't mind talking about the Kelly Kid. 'And I was right, wasn't I?' she added indignantly. 'I saw you laughing at me in the dining hall.'

'That?' Daniel shook his head. 'I laughed because I couldn't believe it was true. I thought someone was trying to play a joke on me! You see, I thought I'd seen you on that Saturday morning quiz show. The one where you win tapes and CDs by answering questions. There's a girl on there who looks just like you.'

'Oh.' Becky looked at her feet. She felt so stupid. And embarrassed, too, because she knew the girl Daniel was thinking of. She was very glamorous. Becky didn't know what to think. Should she be flattered? 'So, are you disappointed that I was only the Kelly Kid?' she asked defensively.

'No!' Daniel roared with laughter. 'To tell you the truth, one of the reasons I wanted to talk to you is because I want to be a TV cameraman when I leave school. And I thought maybe, if you'd been on TV, you could give me some tips.'

'Oh.' Becky felt her happiness burst like a balloon. So he wasn't really interested in her after all.

'I don't know anything about cameras,' she said flatly. It was a lie. She'd often spent the day at the TV studios while her mum was working. She'd watched the camera crews and the things they did. But she didn't feel like telling him that.

Daniel's face fell. 'Oh, that's a shame.' He bent down to check something on his bike, then straightened up again. 'Well, actually – that wasn't the only reason I wanted to talk to you. In a way that was an excuse. I just thought it would be a way of getting to know you.'

Becky looked at him. The great Daniel Armstrong, whom all the girls fancied, was nervous!

'Well, actually I do know a bit about TV,' she admitted, feeling more confident. She could feel the excitement beginning to well up once more. 'My mum's an actress, and I *was* the star of the Kelly's Krunch advert, of course!' They both laughed.

'In that case, I'd like to hear what goes on, if you don't mind talking about it.' He grinned. 'And I'd like to hear more about you, too, of course. Maybe we could go for a pizza later?'

That made Becky jump. 'That would be great,' she said with a nod, 'but I can't come tonight. I'm going out with the others – in fact I'm going to be late,' she added reluctantly. There was nothing she'd like more than to talk to Daniel all evening. 'But I'll see you at school, shall I?'

'I'm sorry you've got to go so quickly. But I'll see you on Monday, in the lunch hour, by the science block. Okay?'

'I'll be there!' Becky waved as she crossed the road. Just let anyone try stopping her!

9

'It's been difficult to decide which two pupils from this class should be in the video,' said Miss Tyler. It was Monday morning and so quiet in the classroom that you could have heard a pin drop. Everyone seemed to be holding their breath.

Miss Tyler wrinkled her forehead. 'There are so many of you who deserve the chance, and I know how disappointed you're going to be. In the end I decided to choose one girl and one boy. I've chosen Clinton Walsh and Becky Burns.'

'Yes!' Becky turned with a huge smile to Liz and Jas. Though Liz congratulated her, Becky felt slightly guilty to see the disappointment in her eyes. It made it difficult for her to feel triumphant, knowing she'd won the place at the expense of her friends.

Loud gasps echoed all round the classroom. There were some shouts of 'No!' and 'Unfair!' and some of the girls burst into tears. Miss Tyler just stood there until everyone had calmed down.

'I'm not going to explain my choices,' she announced when it was quiet. 'All I'll say is that Becky's idea for the fête on Saturday really got the class out of serious trouble, and that Clinton often stays behind after lessons and helps me clear up the workshop, which I appreciate.'

At that moment the bell for the first lesson of the day rang. Miss Tyler looked relieved. 'Off you go, all of you.'

Becky was almost floating on air as she and Jas went down the corridor. 'I can't believe it!' she kept saying, over and over. After all the ups and downs of the last two weeks, the news that she was really going to get her chance to appear with Rory Todd just wouldn't sink in. Jas grabbed her arm and pinched her gently.

'You're not dreaming, Becky! It's real! We're going to meet Rory Todd!'

'I'm getting a sore throat,' Jas complained as she dropped on to the grass beside Charlie. 'All this rehearsing's too much for me.'

'What do the Porcupines sound like?' asked Liz. 'Are they getting any better?' She was making a list of the things she wanted to take away on the adventure weekend.

Jas frowned and pulled out her packet of chewing-gum. 'The boys are improving. They can actually play in tune now. But Kirsty still can't sing. She sounds as if she's shut her fingers in a door.'

'Good,' Becky said sharply. 'I hope the others regret choosing her now.'

'You sound fed up.' Jas looked at her curiously.

'Gina Galloway accused me of sucking up to Miss Tyler to make her choose me.' Becky punched the grass in frustration. 'Whatever I do, it's wrong. I just can't win! If I hadn't done the stall at the fête, we wouldn't have made any money for charity and she'd still be making fun of me. Now she's horrible because she thinks I shouldn't have been chosen for the video.'

'The video's being recorded tomorrow,' Liz pointed out sensibly. 'By Friday she'll have forgotten all about it. Don't worry, Becky.'

Becky rolled her eyes. 'By Friday she'll probably have something new to moan at me about!'

'Well, at the moment I'm more worried about my hair than stuck-up Gina Galloway.' Jas ran her fingers through her crop. 'If I had hair like Charlie's I could do something spectacular. But it's too short to do *anything* with.'

'Come here. Let's try this.' Becky took off the wide stretchy black band she was wearing round her hair and pulled it over Jas's forehead. 'How about this way?'

'No,' Charlie said firmly, 'definitely *not* that way. You look like a Sumo wrestler.'

'Then this way.' Becky adjusted the band.

'Not that way, either,' advised Liz. 'It makes her look like a dangerous criminal.'

'Thanks!' Jas took the band off. 'I don't know what to do. Rory'll be here tomorrow and I can't really get my hair cut any shorter.' She rolled over on the grass.

'You could have your head shaved,' suggested Charlie, who was looking through the latest issue of one of her animal rights magazines. 'You'd certainly catch Rory's eye then.'

'And it wouldn't take long to wash and dry in the morning,' Becky added.

'And my mum would murder me,' Jas finished with a groan.

'You could dye it.' Liz sounded uncertain, but Jas jumped at the idea.

'Yes! I could go blonde. Or I could put henna on it and go—'

'Orange,' supplied Charlie, playing with her own naturally red hair. 'Remember the time Lisa Willis put henna on her hair?'

Jas nodded. 'Mmm, she went tangerine. Maybe I'll forget the henna.'

'How about going strawberry blonde – sort of blonde with a touch of pink?' Becky was diving into her backpack. 'Like Courtney Vale, the girl Rory took to the film première.' She pulled out a magazine. 'There's a feature in here about Courtney Vale and her beauty routine. I'm sure I read about what she puts on her hair to make it that colour.'

Together they looked through the article. 'Here it is,' Becky murmured a minute later. 'She bleaches her hair with Halo bleach and then she mixes up Halo number one dye and number fourteen dye and puts it on for twenty minutes. You could do that. And that colour would look great on you.'

Liz interrupted. 'What'll your parents say? My mum wouldn't be pleased. I didn't really mean you to take it so seriously when I suggested dyeing your hair.'

'But why not?' Becky asked. 'Jas'll look stunning. Once her mum sees how good she looks, she won't mind.'

Jas was reading the article. 'I'm not sure about that, Becky. You haven't met my mum. It's a bit drastic. And what if the colour doesn't suit me? By tomorrow it would be too late to change it.'

'Don't be chicken,' teased Becky. 'I promise, you'll look great.'

'Don't do anything stupid,' Liz advised. 'You'll regret it.'

'Look,' Becky began, 'Courtney Vale's hair is a wonderful colour. And Rory obviously likes girls with hair like that.'

Jas hesitated. 'All right,' she said slowly, 'I'll do it.'

'Brilliant!' Becky exclaimed.

'On one condition – that you dye your hair, too. After all, you want Rory to look at you, too, don't you?'

Becky thought about it. What did she have to lose? Her hair was already blonde. Using a bit of bleach and dye wouldn't make much difference at all.

'Sure,' Becky replied easily. 'I'll meet you at the front gate after school and we'll go straight to the store and get the bleach and dye.'

Liz rolled her eyes, wishing she'd never mentioned it. 'I just hope you two know what you're doing.'

Jas frowned as they walked up the aisles where the hair products were kept. 'They don't do Halo bleach and dye here, either,' she muttered. 'They've got every brand in the world except that one.'

'This is the last shop worth trying.' Becky picked up another brand of bleach. 'Look, what's wrong with this? It'll work just the same as Halo. All it does is take the natural colour out of your hair.' She dropped the bottle into her shopping basket. Jas looked uneasy.

'The bleach may be okay, but what about the colours?'

Becky pulled the magazine from her bag. 'It says here that Halo number one dye is a pale blonde colour and number fourteen is light copper. All we have to do is find two other dyes . . . '

Jas ran her fingers along the packets. She stopped at one called Sun Blonde. 'How about this?'

'Perfect.' Becky threw it in the basket. 'Copper next. Here's something: Pure Copper. That'll do. Courtney Vale, eat your heart out. By the time we've finished, our hair's going to look even better than yours.'

'Yeah,' agreed Jas. 'Come on, race you to the cash desk.'

'It's not exactly the same colour as Courtney Vale's, is it?' Jas peered at herself in the dressing-table mirror. It was more than two hours since they'd arrived at Becky's house and started work on their hair. 'When you mixed the dye I think you put in too much copper and not enough blonde.'

'Maybe. It didn't say how much of each to use, so I just mixed up both tubes. And I don't think we rinsed out all the bleach properly, you know.'

'Now you tell me!' exclaimed Jas.

Becky was still trying to get used to her new appearance. She'd never had sand-coloured hair before. 'Still, it's certainly an eye-catching shade.'

'Mmm,' Jas said uncertainly. 'It's different, I'll admit that. I can honestly say I've never seen anyone else with hair this colour.' She picked up the magazine and read through the magazine article again. 'I know where we went wrong. We left the dye on for half an hour instead of twenty minutes. That probably explains it.'

'And Halo dyes are probably a slightly different

shade.' Becky brushed her hair and tied it back with a band. 'You know, I think I like it,' she said after a while. 'It just takes a bit of getting used to, that's all.'

Jas ran her fingers through her short, gingery locks. 'I know what you mean. It's not what I expected, but it looks pretty good. I feel like a different person now my hair's changed.'

'It looks miles better than it did before,' Becky assured her. 'Rory'll go wild about it, I'm sure.'

'And so will my mum when she sees it.' Jas was suddenly worried. 'If she hates it, she might try and stop me appearing in the video.' She glanced around the room anxiously. 'Have you a hat I could borrow, Becky? If I had a hat I could just slip into the house, say good night and go up to my room. That way she won't know I've dyed my hair till after the video.'

Becky opened one of her cupboards. 'How about this?' She held out a black velvet hat with a floppy brim.

Jas put it on. It came well down over her forehead and hid all her hair. 'Perfect. I can go home safely now. She'll never guess.'

'I'll come and let you out. Hold on a second.' Becky wrapped her own head in a towel and went downstairs with Jas. She felt pretty sure that her father and Susie wouldn't approve of her new look one bit. They'd have to find out sometime, of course – but maybe it would be better if she could keep it a secret till tomorrow evening. After that, it wouldn't matter how furious they were. She'd have memories of Rory to comfort her.

'Bye!' Jas disappeared down the path. 'See you tomorrow.'

Susie came out of the sitting-room, carrying coffee mugs, as she shut the front door. 'Have you and Jas had a good evening?'

'We were just trying out new hairstyles,' Becky said casually. She faked a big yawn. 'I think I'll go up and have an early night. I don't want to have bags under my eyes when Rory arrives.'

Susie gave her a goodnight kiss. 'Sleep well.'

Becky nodded. But the last thing she had on her mind was sleep!

Rory was gazing at her, his face just inches away. She could feel his warm breath on her cheek. 'Becky, darling,' he said in that incredible voice of his, 'I don't just want you to be in my video, I want . . . ' His voice faded in a noise like hailstones.

'Rory?' Becky opened her eyes. Sure enough, Rory's face was just a few inches away – but it wasn't the real Rory, just a picture of him stuck to the wall beside her bed.

She checked the clock on the bedside chest. It was almost seven in the morning. The last thing she remembered she'd been wide awake, about five hours ago, knowing that she wasn't going to get a wink of sleep for thinking about the day ahead. Somehow she must have dozed off.

A rattling noise against the window made her jump. What was happening? Becky drew back the curtain and looked out. In the garden below, a figure wearing a black hat waved furiously back at her. *Jas?* Becky opened the window. 'What are you doing here? It's not seven o'clock yet!'

Jas stared at her strangely. 'I need to see you. Right now! Something terrible's happened,' she cried. 'Come down and let me in.'

Becky threw on her bathrobe and crept down the stairs to the front door. Her dad and Susie would be in bed a little longer, thank goodness. Jas came in silently and raced up the stairs, closing Becky's bedroom door softly as soon as they were both safely inside.

'What is it?' Becky's heart was thumping. 'What's happened? Has your mum found out about your hair?'

Jas was shaking. 'No, it's a million times worse than that!'

Becky's eyes widened. 'What could be worse than that?'

'When I went to bed I couldn't sleep, I was so excited about Rory.'

'Me, too,' said Becky.

'So at six o'clock I got up and tried on the outfit I'm wearing for the video. And when I looked in the mirror . . . '

'What?'

'This.' Jas pulled off the hat.

For a long time Becky just stood there gaping. Jas's hair had turned bright green!

'Don't stand there gulping like a goldfish,' Jas complained. '*Do* something!'

Becky shook her head in disbelief. 'It looks amazing! I know you didn't want green hair, but in some ways it really suits you.' She began to giggle. 'Can you imagine what Miss Tyler is going to say when she sees it?'

Jas looked like thunder. 'Before you start laughing too loudly, you'd better take a look in the mirror yourself.'

Becky turned round, expecting to see her face framed by sandy-coloured hair. 'No!' Her hair was the same shade of green as Jas's. She just stared and stared, while her stomach did somersaults. 'What are we going to do?'

'I was hoping you'd know. After all, you're the one who got us into this mess.'

Becky whirled round. 'That's not fair. You're the one who wanted to change hair colour!'

'And you're the one who thought she knew all there was about it,' snapped Jas. 'Now look what you've done to me!'

'If it wasn't for you wanting to dye your hair, this wouldn't have happened to me!' shouted Becky. They glared furiously at each other.

At last Jas's face softened. 'Let's call it a truce. We can go on arguing about whose fault it is for ever. But that won't solve the problem of what we're going to do about it.'

Becky nodded. 'You're right. Why don't we start by washing it and see if that makes any difference?'

'It doesn't, I've already tried.' Jas looked grave. 'I don't know what to do. It's too late to dye it back to its original colour. We've got to be in school in two hours. And anyway, if we try to bleach it again it'll probably all fall out.'

'We'll have to find some way of hiding it, then. Hats.'

'But we're not allowed to wear hats in class,' Jas pointed out.

'Scarves, then. Are there any rules about scarves?' Becky opened one of her drawers and pulled out a handful.

'Probably,' Jas said darkly. But Becky was already tying a scarf round her head so that it covered all her hair.

'What do you think?'

Jas grunted unenthusiastically, then reached out for a flowery blue one and began to wrap it round her own hair. 'I'm getting desperate,' she confessed. 'So a scarf will have to do.'

Becky inspected herself in the mirror. Jas was right. The scarf didn't look great. But when you had green hair, you had to take desperate measures.

'Where have you two been?' Charlie was looking anxious when Becky and Jas arrived in registration. 'We thought you'd changed your minds about being in the video,' she went on. 'And why are you wearing those scarves?'

'Don't ask, please.' Becky slid into her seat and wished she was invisible. As they'd come up the school drive lots of people had made some smart comment about the scarves. It was driving her mad.

Liz gasped and put her hand to her mouth. 'Oh, no,' she cried. 'You dyed your hair, didn't you?'

Becky nodded. 'Yes. But please don't ask questions.' She wasn't sure she could take any more without bursting into tears. Why did nothing in her life go according to plan?

But there was no time to think about that. Miss Tyler, resplendent in her best red dress and matching shoes, came sweeping in.

'Please don't let her notice,' Jas prayed from her seat behind Becky.

But her prayers weren't answered. 'Scarves off, please, girls,' instructed Miss Tyler, barely glancing at them. 'You know you're not allowed to wear them in school. Not even today.'

Jas looked pale. 'I know we're not allowed to wear hats in class,' she protested, 'but there's no rule against scarves.'

Miss Tyler put her head on one side. 'Why do I have the feeling that something strange is going on?' She walked up the aisle to Becky's desk. 'Please take your scarf off, Becky. You can put it on again after school.'

Becky hesitated. Panic was rising inside her. She didn't know what Miss Tyler would have to say about green hair, but she felt pretty certain she wouldn't like it. If only they'd dyed it red, it might have been okay. She felt desperate – as if she could see her chance of appearing with Rory Todd slipping through her fingers. 'You, too, Jasmine,' insisted Miss Tyler.

Becky and Jas glanced at each other tight-lipped. It was no good. Slowly they unwound the scarves. There was a loud gasp from the class and Gina Galloway squealed with laughter. Even Miss Tyler pursed her lips and stood back in amazement. 'I thought you might have had outrageous haircuts,' she said, putting her hand to her forehead. 'But green hair? Girls, what are you thinking of?'

'It's a mistake,' wailed Jas. 'We were trying to dye our hair the same colour as Courtney Vale's and it went wrong.'

'I'll say it did,' commented Gina nastily. Everyone laughed, except for Miss Tyler, who was frowning.

'I think you'd better put the scarves back on,' she told them, walking back to her table. 'They'll cause less of a commotion around the school than your hair. I'll write you a note saying I've given you permission to wear them. Give it to each teacher at the beginning of your lessons. And I'll have to ask the head teacher to talk to your parents about this. I presume they don't know what's happened?'

Jas and Becky nodded silently. Becky knew that her father and Susie would be furious – but she wouldn't have to see them until this evening. Right now there were more urgent things to worry about.

Miss Tyler drummed her fingers on the table. 'This makes everything very difficult. I don't think you can appear in the video looking like this. The head teacher's anxious to give a good impression of the school. We don't want parents thinking that we encourage pupils to have green hair.'

'But Miss Tyler!' both girls exclaimed. *Please!'*

Becky's eyes began to swim with tears. After everything she'd done – to have it taken away at the last moment like this was too much.

'I'm sorry, girls.' Miss Tyler shook her head regretfully. 'I know it's a terrible disappointment. But you should have been more sensible.'

Jas began to cry. 'I'm sorry,' Becky murmured.

'I wish you'd never come to this school,' Jas snapped. 'Ever since you've arrived there's been nothing but trouble.' She turned away and buried her face in her hands.

Becky couldn't argue. Everything she touched seemed to end in disaster. Why was her life such a big mess?

Miss Tyler faced the rest of the class. 'We'll need to choose another girl to represent the class – someone without green hair.' She surveyed the eager faces, then put her hand to her head. 'Liz Newman – I'm choosing you. I think I can rely on you not to do anything silly.'

Liz had been so busy trying to comfort Becky and Jas that she wasn't paying proper attention. Charlie had to tap her on the shoulder.

'What's wrong with you, Liz?' said Charlie. 'Miss Tyler just selected you to appear with Rory Todd!'

Liz opened her eyes wide with shock. 'Thank you!' she called to the teacher. Then a look of panic crossed her face. 'I don't know if I really want to be in this video,' she said nervously. 'What will I have to do? Oh, I wish Miss Tyler had chosen someone else!'

'Talk about ungrateful,' Becky complained half-jokingly. 'Jas and I would do anything to get into that video – and all *you* can do is try and find a way out of it.' She smiled, trying to make light of it, but it was impossible to hide the terrible disappointment she felt inside.

It was mid-morning break and the first time the girls had had a real chance to talk. 'I'm sorry, Becky.' Liz was still looking shocked. 'I'm just not as outgoing as you are. The thought of appearing on TV makes me nervous. And it's not my fault that you two dyed your hair green. I did warn you.'

While she was speaking, Jas came round the corner of the science block. Her face was white and still streaked with tears. 'What did the band have to say?' asked Charlie, putting an arm round her.

'They're furious with me. They've told me that even when my hair's back to normal, I can forget about being a Porcupine.' Jas blew her nose. 'I can't blame them. Who's going to sing for them now? Kirsty can't do it. Rory Todd would die laughing if she tried.'

'Well they're the last people in the world I feel sorry for,' Becky said flatly. 'If they'd been straight to start with, we wouldn't be in this mess.'

'But the fact is, we are.' Liz sighed.

'And you're the one who got us into it,' Jas accused, looking pointedly at Becky. It was true in a way, thought Becky. If only she hadn't got so carried away with the hair dye everything would be all right. The tears she'd managed to hold back for so long finally broke through.

'I'm sorry.' Becky said, sobbing. And as hard as she tried, no other words came out. Charlie and Liz patted her on the back and Liz took out a clean hanky and gave it to her to dry her eyes.

'Well,' Charlie said when Becky at last stopped crying, 'at least we'll all be able to see Rory. That's better than nothing.'

'Miss Tyler said he's going to talk to the whole school after lunch. Maybe you'll get a chance to meet him after that,' Liz said, trying to sound cheerful.

Becky managed a weak smile. She didn't know what to think or believe, but there was nothing more to lose.

10

'Who *are* all those people?' Becky had never seen the school hall look so crowded.

'The kitchen staff are here, and the caretaker and the secretaries.' Emma laughed. 'Anyone who's got *anything* to do with the school has come along.'

Becky wished they hadn't. It was so crowded she could barely see the stage.

At that moment someone walked out from behind the curtains. For a second there was a cheer. Then everyone realised that it wasn't Rory Todd, just the head teacher. He made a speech about what a wonderful school Bell Street was. 'And now, the man you've all been waiting for,' he announced finally. 'Bell Street's famous pupil, Rory Todd!'

There was deafening applause and cheers as Rory, dressed in jeans and a blue shirt, appeared on stage.

'Rory . . . Rory,' Becky chanted with the others.

Rory came to the front of the stage and held up a hand. He seemed to be in a serious mood. Instantly the hall went silent. 'I'm not going to pretend that I liked coming to school,' he told them. 'But I've returned today because I've got an important message for you and all the other kids out there.'

Becky stared at his gorgeous green eyes. He was every bit as good-looking as his photos. And as he talked, it was as if he were speaking to her alone.

'I've come back to Bell Street because I want to teach all of you about the importance of protecting our planet. We have to look after the world we live in, or in a few generations there'll be nothing left.'

'Isn't he just the most gorgeous guy you ever saw?' Jas whispered rapturously.

Becky nodded. She had a big lump in her throat as she imagined what might have been.

'I'm here today to make the video for my new record, "Green For Life". I wanted to bring the message home to the place I grew up in,' continued Rory. 'And I wanted some of you to appear in the video with me and help spread the news that we all need to be green – not just for our own lives, but for the life of the planet.'

The hall erupted in cheers as Rory finished speaking. He waved to them all and then walked off stage.

'I wonder if he's a vegetarian,' Charlie said when the noise died down.

But Becky and Jas weren't listening. 'I can't believe that was it.' Becky shook her head. 'Is that all we're going to see of him?'

'It looks like it.' Jas stared up at the stage. 'If only . . . ' she murmured.

The head teacher marched out again. 'Now,' he instructed, 'I want everyone except those pupils who have been selected by their teachers to leave the hall and go back to their classes.' There was a huge groan.

'Bye, Liz.' Becky tried to smile bravely at her friend. 'Have a good time with Rory. We'll want

112

to hear all about it later. And get us his autograph if you can.'

'If you get a chance to speak to him, maybe you could explain about the Porcupines and why there's no lead singer,' Jas suggested. 'Tell him that we're his number one fans, will you?'

'I'll try.' Liz looked round nervously, then walked over to join the excited group of students gathered by the stage.

Reluctantly, and with their eyes misty with tears, Becky and Jas joined the line of kids filing slowly out of the hall. It took ages to get to the door and as they did so, Mr Heyward, who was on patrol duty, stopped them.

'Take those silly scarves off your heads, girls. It's no good trying to draw attention to yourselves now. Rory Todd's not going to pick you two for his video.'

'But we have permission to wear them, sir,' Jas explained while Becky tried to find Miss Tyler's note in her pocket.

'I don't care whether you've got permission to fly to Mars!' he snapped, ushering the last few students through the door. 'Just take those things off. You look ridiculous.'

'But Miss Tyler said—'

Their argument was interrupted by noise from the stage. It was Rory Todd, and he was gesturing to the crowd of excited kids waiting in the hall. Spellbound, Becky and Jas turned to watch.

'These kids are all too neat and tidy,' he was insisting to another man who was carrying a clipboard. 'They're just not right for the video.'

'That must be the video director,' whispered Becky.

113

The video director was arguing with Rory now. 'Look, these kids have been specially chosen by the teachers. They're the students who've contributed most to the school. They deserve to be in the video.'

'I don't care.' Rory held up his hand. 'Look, guys, I'm sorry. When I had the idea of filming some of the pupils here I was thinking of the kind of kids who are like me when I was at school. Kids who aren't always sensible. Kids who get into scrapes.'

'Kids like us,' said Becky with heavy irony.

'The video won't work if it's full of squeaky-clean kids,' Rory finished.

Jas raised her eyebrows. 'Liz will hate being called squeaky-clean!' she exclaimed. 'You know how insulted she gets when we tell her how sensible she is.'

Mr Heyward, who'd had his eyes glued to the scene on the stage, turned back to them. 'What did I tell you two?' he asked. 'Take those scarves off this moment.'

'But, sir!' Becky argued, holding out Miss Tyler's note.

'*Now* – or do you want to spend a whole week in detention?' he threatened. The girls looked at each other and shrugged, then slowly began to undo the scarves. As they shook out their hair, Mr Heyward spluttered with surprise. 'What's this? Some kind of joke? Now I understand why Miss Tyler told you to wear the scarves,' he muttered. 'Why didn't you tell me what you'd done?'

'We tried to explain,' started Jas.

'But you wouldn't listen to us,' Becky finished furiously.

Mr Heyward made a tut-tutting sound. 'Well you'd better just put those scarves back on and run along to your next class.'

Becky and Jas turned to take one last look at Rory Todd, then opened the hall doors. They were just about to walk out when a voice froze them in mid-step.

'Stop those girls! I want to see those girls with green hair!'

'Come here, you two!' Becky felt her knees go weak as Rory Todd called them up on to the stage. 'Are you wearing wigs or is that hair for real?' he asked with a gleaming smile. Up close he was even more handsome than in his photos.

'It's real,' Jas said confidently. 'We didn't mean to turn it green. Something went wrong with the hair dye.'

Rory laughed. 'It's perfect! My song is about green issues, so what could be better than having two girls with green hair in the video?'

'But, Rory,' exclaimed the video director, 'we've made plans to have forty kids dancing in the background of the video. And then there's the band. They're supposed to appear in it too.'

Rory shook his head and paced the stage. 'This is a far better idea.'

'But we can't possibly allow these pupils to appear in the video!' spluttered Mr Heyward. 'Our pupils aren't allowed to have green hair. We don't want the public to see them like this.'

'I think it would be a great advert for the school,' Rory countered.

'But what are we going to do with the girls?'

Becky glared at the video director. What was he trying to do – ruin her last remaining chance of stardom?

'Can you sing?' Rory's green eyes stared straight into hers and Becky felt her heart melt.

'Can we sing?' Jas raised her eyebrows in disbelief. 'Of course we can sing!' She nudged Becky who was standing there as if Rory had hypnotised her. 'Shall we sing our version of "Mystery Girl"?'

Becky nodded, emerging from the trance that Rory's eyes had put her into. 'One, two three . . .' Jas counted, and they began their favourite song, which they'd sung so often together in the last week. Even though she was nervous, Becky's voice was sweet and clear. After the first few notes she and Jas gained confidence and started to harmonise.

Becky shut her eyes and imagined she was at home, enjoying herself – not doing the most important audition in her life. Slowly she began to dance the steps she'd practised in front of her bedroom mirror. It felt great. She knew she'd never sung so well before. She felt happier than she'd ever felt.

Rory Todd stood there with a smile on his face, while the video director stood there and fumed and shook his head. There was a long silence as they finished. Then the crowd of kids waiting in the hall began to clap. Rory walked over and put a hand on their shoulders. 'Forget the school band and the other kids. I want these two to be the stars of the video!'

'Look what they've done to the chemistry lab!' It was only a couple of hours since they'd sung for Rory, but it felt like days. They'd been so busy there hadn't been time to think. Becky rubbed her eyes and then wished she hadn't. The make-up lady had given her strict instructions not to touch her face.

Jas stared round. Hundred of test tubes and flasks had been set up along the lab benches, all of them pouring out clouds of coloured smoke. It looked as if the room was full of fog.

'It's supposed to be chemical pollution,' one of the props assistants explained as she hung a plastic skeleton against the blackboard.

'And I suppose that's what'll happen to all of us if we keep poisoning the world,' Becky observed.

'I hope you're not scared of mice,' the props girl asked. 'Because later in the video, you've got to pick up a cage of mice and open the door to let them escape. It's part of the green message. You know, it's cruel to lock animals up and do experiments on them.'

'I don't mind mice,' said Becky. 'And Charlie is going to love this video!'

At one end of the room the technical crew had put up dozens of lights and were focusing their cameras. Jas laughed nervously. 'I hope I'm not going to make a mess of this. We start by dancing between the benches, don't we?'

Becky nodded. 'And when we get to the end, Rory pops up and we dance each side of him and mime the chorus of the song.'

Jas put her hand to her head. 'It's just trying to remember everything! Two hours ago I hadn't even

117

heard of the song, now I'm supposed to know the words by heart.'

'And dance too!' Becky did a few of the steps Rory had shown them. 'But don't worry, they'll keep filming until we get it right.'

At that moment Rory appeared in the lab, ready to begin shooting. He was wearing a green shirt and trousers. 'What do you think, girls?'

Becky giggled. 'We match perfectly!' The suit was the same colour as their hair and the green tops that the wardrobe mistress had given them. They also wore bright red leggings, which Becky loved. 'We're going to have to hide these from Miss Tyler,' she'd told Jas when they'd tried them on.

The video director, who'd got over his bad mood and now seemed to think girls with green hair were quite a good idea, called for silence. 'Girls, get into position. When the music starts and I tell you, start dancing towards Rory.'

Becky and Jas glanced at each other. 'This is really happening, isn't it?' Jas asked as she stood on her spot.

'Yes,' coughed Becky as the make-up lady came up and powdered her nose and chin. Rory Todd was standing just a few metres away, watching and giving them an encouraging smile.

'Okay. Lights on.'

At the director's instruction, all the lights came on. They were so bright the girls were almost blinded. Dry ice fog rose from around their ankles. 'Run VT. Cue music.' The music started loud and clear. Becky and Jas listened for their cue. 'Action!' yelled the director, and they started to dance . . .

'What was he really like?' Liz asked for the hundredth time as 2K crowded into the Media Studies classroom the following week. 'I mean *really*?'

'I told you, he was great,' Becky replied simply.

Liz frowned. 'I still think he's too bossy to be really nice. The Porcupines were furious that he just decided to drop them from the video. So were most of the other kids the teachers had chosen.'

'He was nice to us,' Becky insisted. 'Even when we made mistakes, he didn't get angry.' Though if she was going to be honest, she didn't feel quite as crazy about Rory now as she had before the video. He was a bit too wild for her, and too old. But he was still gorgeous.

'Is he a vegetarian?' Charlie asked. 'Did you ask him?'

'No, I didn't ask him.' Becky sighed. 'But he had a cheese sandwich during the break, so maybe.'

Miss Tyler followed them into the room carrying a video cassette. Jas pulled a nervous face and squeezed Becky's arm. 'Look, that's it! That's the video!'

Even Miss Tyler was looking excited. 'Find a seat everyone,' she instructed, going over to the video machine and sliding the tape into position. 'This is the version of the video you'll all be seeing on TV in the next few weeks. Rory Todd has sent us a copy and the head teacher thought Becky and Jasmine and the rest of the class should be the first to see it.'

Becky crossed her fingers. She remembered what it had been like seeing the Kelly Kid video for the first time and realising what a fool she looked. That wasn't going to happen again, was it?

Miss Tyler pressed the remote control and stood

119

back. The monitor fizzed and then suddenly exploded into sound and colour – and there they were, their green hair amazing under the lights as they danced around the chemistry lab. Everyone gasped.

'They didn't really film that here at school, did they?' Charlie said disbelievingly.

Becky nodded. 'You should have seen Mr Harris's face when he saw what they were doing to his lab!'

There were shrieks and sighs when Rory appeared and began to sing. 'You look so glamorous,' Liz breathed as the camera zoomed in on Becky's face. 'And look at Jasmine's lipstick!'

Jas groaned. 'My mum'll go mad when she sees all that make-up. She still hasn't forgiven me for the hair.' She glanced up and nudged the others. Ryan and Clinton were standing up and had begun to dance.

Becky grinned. 'Let's dance!' She jumped up and joined in. Soon the whole class was dancing. Even Miss Tyler was tapping her foot and humming along.

'It's great! Play it again,' Ryan demanded when the song finished, but Miss Tyler stood firm.

'You'll have the chance to see it as many times as you like over the next few weeks but for now it has to go back to the head teacher's office. And *you* have to go out for mid-morning break.'

But everyone wanted to stay and tell Becky and Jas how great they thought the video was. 'I bet the song goes straight to number one,' Emma insisted. Gina Galloway sniffed disbelievingly, but no one took any notice.

'You know, that green hair really suited you,' said Ryan. 'Why did you have to dye it back to the normal colour?'

'Because my parents went crazy when they saw it,' Becky exclaimed. She could still remember the look of horror on their faces. And even though they grounded her for two whole weeks, Becky couldn't really complain about it.

'What was it like when Rory put his arm round you and danced down the stairs?' Liz asked breathlessly. 'If it was me I would have died.'

'It was great,' Becky giggled. 'But I was so nervous about falling down the stairs I hardly noticed Rory!'

Jas looked over to Becky with a special grin. 'It's the best video ever! And if it hadn't been for you and your crazy idea about dyeing our hair, it wouldn't have been nearly so good. I'm sorry I said your ideas got us into nothing but trouble.'

Becky laughed. 'That's okay. I felt pretty bad about it too. But it's good to know that sometimes my ideas aren't so crazy after all.'

'It's going to seem really quiet here now all the excitement's over.' Liz was sitting with the rest of the gang in their usual secluded spot at the edge of the playing field. They'd spread out their books and were supposed to be preparing for the lesson after lunch, but not much studying was being done.

'Life just isn't going to seem the same without Rory Todd,' Charlie said with a sigh. She lay on her back and her glasses glinted in the sun. 'Maybe he'll come again and do his next video here.'

Liz groaned and shook her head. 'I couldn't bear all that tension again!' Her hair band fell off and Jas, who'd just arrived, sat down on it.

'Ouch!' She handed it back. 'There must be lots of

things for us to look forward to.' She thought about it for a minute. 'No, not many, really.' Her glance strayed across the playground to a tall, dark-haired figure talking to some other boys. 'But at least we'll have someone to gossip about, won't we, girls? Will it be true love or just a passing romance?'

Becky kicked Jas indignantly. 'It's true love, of course!'

Liz put down the essay she'd just been checking and followed her gaze. 'Oh, you mean Daniel Armstrong!'

Becky laughed and rolled over. 'Daniel says he understands and doesn't mind waiting until my parents let me out again. So at least I can think about going out with him. And my friends are coming up from London to stay for the weekend, so that'll be great. How about all of us getting together? Maybe we could have a party.'

'That would be great!' Jas exclaimed. 'And we can find out whether you were crazy at your old school, or whether it's just something Bell Street's done to you!'

'Maybe we could all dye our hair blue,' Becky suggested. 'That would liven things up a bit.'

'No, thanks,' Jas cried. The others laughed.

'Don't forget the adventure weekend coming up,' said Charlie. 'Everyone's going on that.'

'Except for poor old Emma,' Liz said. 'She never does anything like that.'

Becky looked puzzled. 'But I'm sure I heard her telling Miss Tyler she was going on the trip.'

'Yeah,' said Charlie, sitting up. 'I heard her too.'

Liz frowned. 'But Emma's parents never let her do anything like that.'

122

'Well, she's going,' Becky said flatly.

Liz shook her head. 'Well, that's very strange. I've got the feeling that girl's up to something . . . '

Find out what Emma is planning in I'm No Angel *the second book in the Bell Street School series.*

Watch out for more books in the Bell Street School series!

I'M NO ANGEL
by Holly Tate

Bell Street School 2

When the school arranges an adventure week-end for 2K, Emma Pennington is certain of one thing – her parents will never let her go. When she was young she had a lot of health problems – and though she's fine now, her parents still want to keep her wrapped in cotton wool.

But Emma's tired of being treated like a baby. This time she's going to do what *she* wants . . .

Watch out for more books in the Bell Street School series!

MYSTERY BOY
by Holly Tate

Bell Street School 3

Liz Newman is up to something. It all starts when class 2K wins the good conduct prize: a trip to Fantasy World, the great new theme park. But Liz suddenly announces that she may not be going – and she won't say why. Then she starts disappearing after school and telling fibs about what she's been doing, and when Becky, Jas and Charlie ask her what's going on, she starts to avoid them. Is Liz seeing someone? Her friends are determined to find out . . .

DEAR CLARE, MY EX BEST FRIEND
by Ursula Jones

Dear Clare,
    What's Australia like? Do you go surfing every day after school? Nothing has happened in England since you left except the usual tons and tons more pollution . . .

But a very great deal is just about to happen to 13-year-old Anna Pitts. Over the next few months, she will fall in love, move to the country, become a vegetarian and a hunt saboteur (nearly), acquire a new grandmother, a hamster and a chicken, fall in love again, get a job, and learn to kiss, all while keeping up a lively correspondence with numerous world leaders about the environment. And write to her best friend Clare, newly emigrated to Australia, to tell her all about it.

'Anna Pitts, aged 13 going on 113, is a feisty commentator on life in an off-the-wall, one-parent, muesli, macramé and madness family. Funny, wry and all too probable, her letters make Adrian Mole look like Violet Elizabeth Bott.'

Maureen Lipman

MORE GREAT BOOKS AVAILABLE
FROM KNIGHT